Shield
Maiden

First published 2016 by Bloomsbury Education,
an imprint of Bloomsbury Publishing Plc

50 Bedford Square, London, WC1B 3DP

www.bloomsbury.com

Bloomsbury is a registered trademark of Bloomsbury Publishing Plc

A CIP catalogue for this book is available from the British Library

ISBN: 978-1-4729-1862-8 (paperback)

Typeset by Newgen Knowledge Works (P) Ltd., Chennai, India
Printed and bound by CPI Group (UK), Croydon CR0 4YY

1 3 5 7 9 10 8 6 4 2

STUART HILL

Shield Maiden

BLOOMSBURY EDUCATION
AN IMPRINT OF BLOOMSBURY

LONDON OXFORD NEW YORK NEW DELHI SYDNEY

The Danish Great Army marched over the land, rank on rank in perfect step, shield overlapping shield like the scales of a dragon. The warriors' helmeted heads were as closely grouped as studs in an armoured gate and over them all flew the feared Raven banner said to make any force that carried it invincible. Not since the time of the Romans had such a disciplined and well-trained army marched through the land, and not since the time of the Romans had so many died trying to stop such an invincible force.

Waiting for them on the wide, flat plain stood the Saxons. At their centre was the king with his small war band of trained professional soldiers, known as housecarles. Around stood the fyrd, part-time fighters who practised with weapons for a day or so each month.

The cry went up from the Danes as they spotted their enemy, and they sang a fierce rolling song that marched with the rhythm of their step. The Saxon king gave the order and his soldiers raised a shield wall and waited, filling the air with their war cries.

Arrows and throwing axes began to fly back and forth, landing to rattle amongst the ranks or thud into flesh and bone. Screams were added to the war cries and the line of fighters began to ebb and flow as warriors fell on both sides and others stepped forward to fill the gaps in the wall of shields. The iron-tinged scent of blood began to rise up over the battlefield.

But still the Saxons held their position and still the Great Army marched on. Now both sides were in closer range and spears began to fly between the two.

The armies were soon near enough to see the faces of those they must kill, and arrows and axes and spears brought down more and more. The fyrd expanded and contracted like a huge cloudbank before a wind, but the king and his band of housecarles stood solid, waiting for the onset of shield on shield.

The space between the enemies closed and now with a roar the Great Army rose up on to its toes and charged. It smashed into the wall like a storm wave hitting a headland. The Saxons fell in their hundreds. The earth beneath them soaked up their blood.

The housecarles held the line with their king, toe to toe with the Danes; axe and sword hacked and clattered down on the enemy. Neither gave way; neither could move forward. Those behind pressed close, while those in the front rank fought for their lives, thrusting and chopping and blocking. The day was filled with the stench of sweat and blood. The roar and screech of metal on metal and wood on wood rose up into the air. The battle song echoed across the sky.

Then with a great heaving shout the Danes rolled forward over the Saxon line, breaking the shield wall. All was in chaos, the ground wet with blood, but the Saxons still fiercely resisted and tried to regroup. The fyrd fought on, charging again and again, dying in their hundreds on the hedge of spears. The Great Army rolled on – unstoppable, unbreachable, unbreakable – bringing death on all who came near.

The fyrd despaired and began to fall back in ones and twos, then in groups and finally in great crowds that turned and ran in a desperate rout that left their king to fight alone with his housecarles. But now the royal war band fell like leaves from wind-blown trees before the storm of Danish steel, until at last the king stood alone.

The Danes caged him in a hedge of spears and, when he dropped his sword, they took him before their leader, who nodded and smiled as his men slit open the king's tunic, laid him on the ground and then chopped a hole in his back and spread his lungs wide to form the 'blood eagle'.

So it was that Aella, Saxon King of Northumbria, died his brutal death.

I

My childhood ended in the town of Chippenham on Christmas Day in the year of our Lord 876. We'd gone to church before the sun had come up and given ourselves to God as was proper and right when we remembered the birth of Christ. The praying and singing had finished, the incense had drifted away, and now the time would be ours.

As a family we walked from the church in procession, as humbly as it was possible for the Royal House of Cerdinga to do. I suppose we all look much alike; I'm the eldest, Aethelflaed, daughter of King Alfred of Wessex, and Edward, my brother, was born a year after me. We're told we look like twins and I've heard us described as having golden hair and eyes like sapphires, with flawless skin and perfect features. At least that's what the chamberlains and other servants say but I suppose they would say that, wouldn't they? Ara, our nurse, doesn't really care about flattering anyone and she says we have mousey hair, eyes as pale as ponds under a winter sky and skin like waxy candles. She's always honest, even when you don't want her to be.

Aethelgifu, the next eldest, looks just the same as us, but she keeps her hair covered most of the time, and then there's little Aethelfryth. She's still very young and I think she really could have hair like spun gold and eyes like sapphires by the time she grows up.

We children had been herded together by our nurse and forced to walk in two pairs. As the eldest, Edward and I went first, smiling and doing our best to behave as royal children were supposed to do after an early-morning service in church. But this didn't last long; we couldn't resist teasing Aethelgifu ... She was so *holy* and good, she even enjoyed the boring parts of a church service, which meant nearly all of it.

"Do you think angel burps sound like bells?" Edward suddenly asked, casting a glance at our younger sister.

This took me by surprise and I snorted loudly. "No, angel burps probably sound like choirs singing!"

We began to giggle at this but an angry voice behind us interrupted and we turned to see Aethelgifu glaring at us, just as we'd hoped. "That's sinful talk! Angels don't ... do that sort of thing!"

"I bet they would if they ate peas and onions," said Edward, warming to our usual game of upsetting our sister. "I can't stop burping when we have those!"

I watched as Aethelgifu went an interesting shade of angry pink. "No, they wouldn't! Angels can eat anything without ... without making any sort of noise."

"How?" I asked, genuinely interested. "Does God stop them burping?"

Aethelgifu's pink face deepened to a blazing red. "Don't you know *anything*? Angels don't have bodies like we do; they're spirits of God! They only make themselves look like people when they bring messages from heaven."

"Well if I was an angel I'd want to burp," said Edward. "In fact when I brought my messages from heaven I'd announce my arrival with a huge echoing burp, like the heralds announce the arrival of a king."

"Don't be ridiculous!" said Aethelgifu. "Haven't you seen the carvings in church? Angels carry trumpets to announce themselves – it's far more seemly!"

"What're you talking about?" asked Aethelfryth, who'd been walking along quietly and trying to listen to our conversation over the cheering of the crowds.

"Never you mind!" said Aethelgifu and glared at us in warning to say nothing else that might corrupt the mind of the little girl.

Edward and I carried on in silence, nudging each other and enjoying a job well done. This was one of the few occasions when my brother and I worked at anything together; usually we were rivals, competing to be the best at almost anything you'd care to mention. The fact that he was a boy might have had something to do with this: although I was older, he was the one who would probably be chosen as the next ruler of Wessex after my father. Girls don't rule countries; they just marry the rulers ... if they're lucky.

Ahead of us marched the housecarles, the soldiers and the palace guards. Their shields were slung on their backs and their swords stayed in their scabbards in honour of the fact it was Christmas Day. They even carried their spears with the heads pointing earthwards in deference to Christ, the Prince of Peace.

Anyway, we continued our procession through the streets, past the wooden houses with their thatched roofs and stout wooden doors that were interrupted here and there with the stone-built structures that had survived from the time of the Romans. The people of the town lined the route and waved and cheered as we passed and soon the sun rose into a polished blue sky. It was a cold winter that year, more snow than rain, more ice and penetrating frosts than mud. We children walked with my father and mother, the king and queen, along the path that had been dug through the deep snow. With us were the thegns, or lords, who helped to rule the country and command the army. Their ladies also joined us and, as we were all dressed in our very best clothes and wearing our most expensive jewels, we glowed and glittered like a bright garden in the winter snow.

Ahead I could see the huge gates that led into the palace precinct. They stood open and the guards thumped their spears on the ground as we walked through. It took quite a while for everyone to file into the courtyard, and then, when the last thegn and his lady had squeezed into the wide space, my father stood looking at the complex of buildings before him, smiling and relaxed, for all the world as though it was a warm spring day instead of icy mid-winter.

The delicious smells of baking and roasting that rose up from the kitchens mingled with the spicy aroma of wood smoke to make a perfume of the day. I looked at the mead hall's brightly painted wooden beams and its roof, neatly covered in red tiles that had been carefully salvaged from Roman buildings. The palace at Chippenham was one of my father's favourites. Here in this mead hall he would hold feasts for his thegns and their soldiers, and it was here that he'd commend bravery in battle and loyalty in service and, as the name suggests, huge amounts of mead and many other sorts of drink were taken.

As this was my father's favourite palace he'd obviously decided that he wanted to enjoy looking at its well-built beauty. So we all stood there in the freezing-cold sunshine, the snow trampled to ice beneath our feet while my father beamed happily at the building before him, waiting until he finally gave the word that would allow us to go into the hall and begin the celebrations. Then a strange figure in black rags stepped from the press around us and placed a hand like a claw on my father's arm.

"Are you waiting for someone to die of cold before you let the rest of us into your mead hall, Alfred King of Wessex?"

Only Ara would have dared to talk to my father like this. As I've already said, she was our nurse, and not only did she seem to be as ancient as the land my father ruled, but she'd also been *his* nurse when he was a little boy. He looked surprised for a moment, but then, seeming to rouse himself from whatever thoughts had been occupying him, he raised his hand. The party of neatly dressed chamberlains who stood before the huge wooden doors swung them open, and a glittering, fire-lit, candle-lit, torch-lit space opened up before us.

In the centre of the wide flagstone floor the fire roared in its deep, pit-like hearth, where the traditional Yule log blazed. It threw dancing shadows and flickering light over the richly worked tapestries that hung over every scrap of wall space.

As king, my father led the way into the hall. We were all so excited we couldn't resist running ahead, and we raced over the flagstones screaming and laughing as we went. I felt I was flying as my cloak billowed behind me and I was almost convinced that I could soar up to the huge brightly painted beams that stretched from wall to wall and held up the high roof.

The hall soon filled with thegns, and their soldiers and ladies, their voices rising to fill the cavernous space with conversation, laughter and the excitement of Christmas. All around us the walls were decorated with the traditional evergreen branches of holly and ivy, which filled the air with a sweet, spicy smell. Then, as the servants rushed forward with jugs, the scent of mulled wine mingled with the foliage to make the proper perfume of Christmas.

My father and mother took their places at the high table that stood at the very top of the hall, and as they sat, so did everyone else, filling the long benches and tables that stood in rows on either side of the huge central fire. Christmas was one of the few occasions that we got to spend time with our parents. Usually Father was too busy with whatever it is kings do when they run countries to have much time for us. And my mother ran the palaces of the royal court like a general commands an army. The chamberlains and servants probably saw more of our mother throughout the year than we did. The only time we could be certain of seeing her was when we'd done something wrong, and then she would descend to hand out punishment.

In fact we children had already been reined in today by some of Mother's special sharp stares and by the even sharper words and hands of Ara. The old nurse was standing in the shadows at the edge of the mead hall and watched us where we were sitting, a little further down the table from our parents. I'd been placed next to Aethelgifu, because she was quiet and it was hoped she'd calm me down. Aethelfryth sat beyond her, and then Edward. He was as wild as me, so once again we'd been deliberately separated. Even so, we grinned at each other over our sisters' heads, and managed to discuss the incoming guests under the covering rumble and chatter of people greedily looking forward to all the eating and drinking.

He suddenly pointed down into the hall. "Look, Aethelflaed, there's Cerdic. I'm surprised he's not training the housecarles even if it is Christmas."

I looked down into the press of people and immediately spotted the old warrior. Cerdic

Guthweinson was the commander of Father's personal guard and even though he was off duty and carrying no weapons he still looked like the soldier he was.

"Do you think he'll allow me to start using a full-sized shield soon?" Edward went on. "I can lift one easily now."

"So can I," I immediately pointed out, not wanting my brother to think he could do something that I couldn't. "We'll both ask him when we begin training again after the Holy Day."

Cerdic's long white hair and beard made him easy to spot in the crowd. He stood as straight as a spear and was easily as strong as the younger housecarles. I only hoped that I'd still be a tough fighter when I was his age.

"Perhaps we should keep ourselves alert and ready for anything, like proper warriors," Edward said, interrupting my thoughts. Then grabbing a winter-stored apple from the large bowl that stood in front of us, he threw it at me. "Here, catch! Stay awake!"

I caught the apple and threw it back, making him dive halfway across the table to scoop it from the air. The duel went on for a happy few minutes, each throw getting wilder and wilder, until finally the apple hit Aethelgifu on the head.

Ara swept down on us like an angry raven, took the apple away and clipped Edward and me round the ear.

"You're the children of the House of Cerdinga, not the peasant brats of some swineherd! Behave like the nobility you are!"

"We're keeping ourselves battle-alert," I answered. "That's *exactly* how Saxon nobility should behave."

Ara turned her icy stare on me, but then she surprised me by nodding sharply as she accepted my argument. "Then do it without killing your sister and without bringing ridicule down on your noble family."

I was the eldest child and so was expected to behave better than the others, even though I rarely did. Just because I was older didn't mean I was more sensible. Why should it? Some of the worst-behaved people I know are grown-ups. Look at Guthrum, King of the Vikings! But in the end I nodded and Ara went back to perch in the shadows at the edge of the hall.

By this time most of the guests had found their places at the long tables and after a dramatic pause the great doors were suddenly flung open. The traditional roasted boar was carried in on a huge metal platter held above the helmets of the escorting housecarles. Everyone cheered wildly and sang the old Yuletide song as it was paraded around the hall.

Now the feast could really begin, and the chamberlains and scullions came running in with tray after tray of food and huge jugs of wine and beer and mead.

The celebrations wore on throughout the day, and the strange thing was, after an early burst of energy and huge noise, the adults seemed to get slowly quieter and more tired with every new dish of food and every beaker of wine. The musicians, who'd been playing energetically when we'd first walked into the hall, were now producing quiet little tunes that meandered up into the roof space along with the smoke from the great central fire. Even Father, who was usually the most talkative and excitable of people, was reduced to murmuring quietly to my mother.

By the time darkness fell some of the guests had slipped under the tables and were snoring loudly, and the rest picked listlessly at yet more platters of food. Ara also seemed to have withdrawn further into the shadows that haunted the edges of the hall and might have been asleep ... if, that is, she did sleep. This of course gave me and my brother and sisters free rein, and soon we were running amongst the tables, laughing and shouting in excitement.

Even some of the housecarle guards, who were supposed to be on duty and not drinking, visibly winced as Aethelfryth's high-pitched voice reached a particularly piercing note when we chased her down the hall.

All of this noise and excitement meant that at first we didn't notice the sounds from outside. They seemed to be coming from the town beyond the palace precinct, and when eventually I stopped running and stood to listen, I could hear dogs barking and what sounded like people screaming. The sound slowly got louder, as though it was coming this way, and suddenly I felt the cold hand of fear touching my shoulder.

Ara appeared beside me as though out of thin air, and without worrying about etiquette or the presence of royalty, she raised her hands. "Listen!" she shouted. "There's movement in the night air! Something stalks the town around us!"

An almost complete silence fell in the mead hall, so that I could hear the Yule log crackling and snapping in the great central hearth. By this time, most of the housecarles had managed to shake off some of the sleepiness caused by the beer, and they slung their shields on their arms and levelled their spears at the huge double doors.

Screams and shouts could now be heard clearly, and suddenly my father shook his head as though to clear it and then leapt over the top table and gave a great shout that called his thegns and soldiers to attention.

"TO ARMS! TO ARMS! THE DANES ..."

But his voice was drowned out by a great splintering crack as the mead hall's doors were broken open and Vikings poured through in an unstoppable gushing rush of axes, swords and spears!

The housecarles charged, locking shields and trying to hold back the enemy. But it was impossible; they were smashed aside and then my father took the kind of instant decision that had made him such a good king. He ran to where we children were and somehow managed to pick three of us up bodily while Ara dragged Edward along by his arm. Father seemed to have the strength of ten as the massive panic and raging fear engulfed the Christmas celebrations.

He ran for the small door that was hidden behind a tapestry at the far end of the hall. He leapt on the top table, knocked over his chair, roared at my mother to run and kicked open the door.

In the mead hall everything was in chaos. People screamed in fear and agony as the Danes rampaged on, killing and maiming as they surged through the room. All the housecarles were dead, and the guests were trying to fight back using whatever came to hand. I watched one old thegn smash his tankard into the face of a Viking, and then stab another with a meat skewer. But it was hopeless; we'd been taken completely by surprise. The palace and town were already lost.

Behind us I could see Ara and also Cerdic Guthweinson, who had a sword and shield he must have picked up from a dead housecarle and was managing to run backwards at an amazing speed as he covered our retreat.

We burst out into the icy, clear night. The stars glittered above us giving all the light we needed as Father kicked his way into the nearby stables. He leapt on to a horse without saddle or bridle, shouted at my mother to do the same and then dragged Edward and me up with him. He watched as Cerdic put Aethelgifu up with Mother and then, after Ara had mounted and taken Aethelfryth up with her, the old soldier finally climbed on to a horse himself.

We erupted into the night like a cavalry charge. The Danes were already in the yard and rushing towards us. Father rode down two, and then we were through the precinct gates and into the town.

Everything was in flames, a choking stench of burning thatch and worse was everywhere, and the streets were heaving with Danes. Father had also picked up a sword and he used it to hack and slash a path through the roaring, raging faces that thrust up before us.

I didn't have time to be afraid. I just wished I had a sword too! Time seemed to slow as our horses ploughed their way through the chaos of fighting bodies and blazing buildings. Then at last the gates of the town loomed before us and our horse reared and struck down a Viking warrior with its hooves. The gates had been smashed open so we shot out into the night, and now the horses had a clear road they galloped forward at great speed.

I looked around me and could see Mother and Ara still riding with us, and each had their small passenger with them. I was amazed to see that Mother had a spear and its blade was bloody, but then the moon rose up over the horizon, bathing the dark world in its subtle cold light, and I saw her face. I realised and remembered then that she was a warrior too, a warrior queen from the ancient Royal House of Mercia. Like all noble women of both Wessex and Mercia, she would have been trained to use weapons just like the men. Though a queen was rarely expected to use them.

We galloped on through the night, the wind roaring in my ears and drowning out the sound of the dying town behind us. At last, after what seemed like half a night of riding, the horses could carry on no more and Father waved us to a stop. The Danes hadn't followed us and we could hear nothing but the horses' snorts as they gulped down air. We all dismounted and, while Father, Mother and Cerdic immediately began to discuss the terrible situation we found ourselves in, we children gathered together in a twittering knot.

"What's going to happen now?" Edward demanded. "Everything's gone!"

He was right. Every certainty we'd ever known had been swept aside. Our home was lost to the Vikings. We'd seen people killed in the streets; we'd watched Chippenham burning as we fled. And though we were young, we knew enough of the dangerous world we lived in to understand that Father was no longer king ... at least he was no longer a king with any power. We didn't even know if Wessex still existed as a separate land in its own right.

As the eldest I felt I had to say something to give us all hope. "Everything may be lost, Edward, but that doesn't mean we can't get it back. It's now that we begin to fight."

I don't think I really believed what I was saying, but at least it sounded good. I did my best to look determined and angry rather than scared.

"How the strong are made weak," Aethelgifu said quietly. "Only this morning we were celebrating Christmas in the Royal Chapel, prince and princesses of the kingdom of Wessex, and now we have nothing but the clothes we're wearing and the horses that brought us to safety. Only God is unchanged in this changeable world."

We all fell silent as though we only now understood the terrible situation we were in. "So where was God when this happened?" Edward suddenly asked. "Why didn't he stop it? And why didn't he save Chippenham from the pagan Danes?"

Aethelgifu looked at him steadily. "No one can understand the plans of God," she said.

The only certainty in all that chaos was Ara. She stood with us in that freezing night, an unchanging presence who'd been with us for as long as any of us could remember. Her black clothing hid most of her form in the shadows, but we could feel her presence like heat beating in pulses into the cold air. I looked at her face as she glared back down the road we'd just ridden along. I was reminded of a piece of carved stone that had been weathered by so many long, harsh winters that the original shape could hardly be seen, and I tried to guess just how old she was.

But then we heard the sound we'd been dreading: galloping hooves!

"Quick, into the trees," Father ordered, and we scrambled off the road and into the shadows of the woods.

Cerdic and Father wrapped cloaks around their left arms to act as rough shields and as one we stared back along the road, which was brightly lit by the full moon. But Ara raised her head to the sky and sniffed, like a hunting dog. "I smell only Saxon blood in living veins. The enemy is too busy looting your palace, Alfred King of nothing but shadows."

We all of us knew that Ara was one of those who still followed the old religion: for her, Christ was a latecomer who was trying to take Woden's crown as king of the gods. We also knew that she had certain ... *powers* that she could sometimes use when they were needed.

Father looked at her sharply, but before anything could be said, the horses thundered into view. One of our own mounts let out a whinny before we could stop it and the group of riders skidded and slid to a halt on the frozen road. They all carried drawn swords and some had shields. If they weren't Saxons we were dead!

"Who's there?" one of them shouted in our language and we sighed with relief. Ara had been right!

My father stepped out of the trees. "Alfred of Wessex. Identify yourselves."

There was an immediate scrambling from the horses and the men knelt with bowed heads. "My Lord, we thought you dead."

"Not yet, and by God's will, not for some years. How many are you?"

The men didn't know, but after a quick head count we established that there were twenty-five altogether. One or two were actually thegns who'd managed to fight their way out of Chippenham, but most were young housecarles who'd fought for as long as they could and then when they saw the situation was hopeless had fled.

Father said nothing against them about this: after all that was exactly what we'd done. To stay and fight against such overwhelming numbers would have meant certain death. Far better to retreat and live to fight back when you were prepared and ready.

But now we had to decide what to do and where to go. This didn't actually take long because everyone who lived under the threat of the Danish Great Army had plans for escape if they attacked. Anyone who didn't have such plans would die.

II

Soon we were back on the road, and this time the pace was a brisk trot to save the horses. It had been decided to go to Athelney, an island in the marshes of Somerset. Its name means the island of 'aethlings' or princes. It was a small royal hunting estate where my father and his brothers had spent a lot of their boyhoods netting wildfowl and fishing. The Danes wouldn't know it and it was so well hidden amongst the reed beds, streams and rivers of the marshlands that only a few locals knew the single causeway that would take you safely through the treacherous mud and waters to its firmer ground.

Ara thoroughly approved of this hideout. She saw the marshes and other wild places of the land as the refuge of the old gods. Here she believed their power was undimmed, hidden from the searching light of the new god from the east.

We trotted on through the night, the clear sky causing the temperature to drop like a stone. A thick rime of frost covered every twig on every tree and coated the already snow-covered ground with deeper layers of ice. The horses' breath smoked on the air and we shivered in our totally impractical best party clothes.

Cerdic had thought to grab blankets from the stables when we'd taken the horses, but there were nowhere near enough to go round. Some of the young housecarles had cloaks and were kind enough to give them to my mother and to us children. But even so, we were still cold.

The horses kept up the pace all night and we ate up the road in front of us. Luckily the icy temperatures meant that any mud on the roads was frozen solid and we made good progress. When the sun rose on the new day, we were miles away from Chippenham, and there was still no sign of pursuit.

I don't think I'll ever forget the glittering glory of that winter's dawn. As the sun rose over the distant horizon of the flat lands we were riding through, a great shimmer and sparkle seemed to rise up from the earth to greet it. Across the wide sweep of frozen land brilliant rainbows, struck from the ice crystals of frost and snow, rose in a cold cascade of colours. And the sky was a wide sweeping wash of blues and pinks and golds that were more beautiful even than the illuminated manuscripts that were made by the holy brothers of the monasteries my father had built.

We stopped for breakfast, but had to wait while some of the housecarles went to get it. Two or three of them had small hunting bows and they crashed off through the reeds that were already beginning to line the road. At some point during the night, we'd crossed the border into Somerset and, not long after, the trees that had been there throughout our journey began to give way to reed beds and a network of streams and small rivers. We stood on the very edge of the great marshes that would be our hiding place.

As we waited Father, Mother and two of the older thegns agreed it was safe to light a fire, as long as we weren't actually on the road itself, and we withdrew into the reeds until we found a small area of fairly dry and flat ground.

Ara shepherded us children along and made sure we had a good place as close to the warming fire as was safe.

"The last time we saw fire it was burning Chippenham to the ground," said Edward miserably.

"Well that was then and this is now, and these flames are warm and friendly," I answered, determined to show my brother that I was stronger than him, and also to be positive for as long as I could.

"This is a test, you know," Aethelgifu suddenly said. She looked at us with the sort of expression she sometimes got when in church and the priest's voice mingled with the incense and the singing in a way that made your head spin. "God's testing our faith, and we must show Him how strong we are by facing this misfortune without complaining."

"If you like," I said, happy to accept anything that would give us the ability to keep going.

"Well I'm complaining," said Edward. "I'm cold and hungry and homeless. Yesterday I was prince of one of the most powerful kingdoms in the country, and now I'm just a tramp wandering the roads!"

Aethelfryth began to snivel as Edward moaned. The cold and the shock of what we'd been through in the last few hours was just too much for such a little girl to bear. But before I could say or do anything to try and cheer her up, Ara swept down on us and glared at her fiercely – and then produced from somewhere under her ragged clothes Aethelfryth's favourite doll. The little girl screamed in delight and hugged the doll close.

"Look after Edith, little one," Ara said in a voice like a calling raven. "She's frightened and not as strong as you. You must keep her safe."

Aethelfryth immediately dried her eyes and then nodded determinedly. She had someone else to think about now, and so was less frightened than she had been.

I looked closely at our ancient nurse. How long had she had the doll? When did she find the time to pick it up in the scramble to escape Chippenham? But before I could ask any of these questions, Ara had withdrawn from my little sister as though something more important was pressing. At first I was afraid that she sensed the Danes were nearby, but there was no real atmosphere of danger about her and I quietly watched as she stood alone at the edge of the reed beds, staring up at the sky. I knew that something strange was going to happen. I could almost feel the air changing around the old woman as she suddenly raised her arms and then threw them wide so that she looked even more like a raven; the black rags of her clothing were like feather-covered wings in the early-morning light.

After a few moments I realised that Ara was quietly chanting, the whispering words blending and tangling with the softly sighing wind that moved through the reeds. Slowly the sound grew until her voice began to wind itself around the campfires. Everyone stopped to stare and my father stood as though he was going to stop whatever was going on. But my mother gently laid her hand on his arm and he paused and instead watched the old woman intently.

I followed Ara's eyes to where they were staring into the cold blue sky and there I saw two tiny black specks. They were so far away I thought they were just birds flying off to begin their day of food-finding. But as I watched, their forms grew larger and clearer and suddenly I knew they were flying directly towards us.

Ara now raised her voice and shouted into the freezing air, "Raarken! Ranhald! Come to me!"

I gasped: they were the names of two wild ravens that sometimes came to her call. They were as black as a moonless midnight and their eyes glinted like polished jet when they caught the light. Once I'd secretly watched Ara standing over a brazier whose smoke seemed to coil and roll into the shapes of living, moving animals as she muttered under her breath, and her ravens had stood on her shoulders and softly croaked and mumbled as though helping with the spell. They were obviously magical birds, but surely even they couldn't have followed us from Chippenham ...

The two birds were so close now that we could hear their raucous cries, and soon they circled high above us in a slowly descending spiral. At last the female raven, Ranhald, landed on the ground before Ara's feet, and Raarken, the male, settled on her shoulder in a rattling clatter of wings. He gently nibbled her ear and crooned softly to her. He was easily the tamest of the two, and when I'd mentioned this in the past to Ara she'd said with a small superior smile:

"Males are always more biddable." But then she'd paused before adding, "And more loyal. Remember that."

I didn't agree with her then, and I still don't. But it has to be said that Raarken was the most friendly. I looked now at the raven as he continued to croon in her ear, almost as though he was giving her information. And perhaps he was, because Ara suddenly turned to where my father stood watching and said, "The Danes aren't bothering to look for you, Alfred, King of no land. They think you're beaten and finished, and won't waste time and effort on trying to capture you."

I could see the rage in my father's eyes as she said this and I still don't know to this day whether it was directed at his old nurse or the enemy.

"It's up to you to prove them wrong, Alfred, once King of Wessex."

Ranhald and Raarken now rose up into the air calling raucously and the soldiers who'd been watching in silence all stood and turned to look at my father.

"We ride for Athelney," he said with quiet force. "From there will begin the first steps of our return."

This simple statement was greeted with an accepting quiet. The king had made his pronouncement. It would be fulfilled.

Not long after that we were dousing the fires and heading back to the road. Once again the horses kept up a swift trotting pace that ate up the miles. Soon we left the last forests and woodlands behind as we travelled deeper into the Somerset Levels. Trees here, when you saw them at all, lined the rivers and ditches and had few branches. Instead they had tangles of long twigs at the top of short trunks so that they looked like bushes growing on top of sticks. Ara told me they were 'pollards' and that people had cut them like that so they could use the wood for fuel and for making things without actually killing the tree.

Apart from that, I don't remember many other details of that journey, only the cold and the fact that we slept under the stars more often than under a roof. We were like the tribes I'd been told about who spend their entire lives travelling, never staying long in one place before moving on to the next. But they lived in lands that were hot and without water, or so I'd been told by teachers my father trusted, so I believed it to be true. I couldn't quite believe that I'd ever be warm again and I envied those travellers and their deserts of burning sands.

Most of the few people we met melted away into the wide reed beds as soon as we appeared. We numbered more than thirty and all of us were on horses, in one way or another. Many of us were armed and, in that empty place of wide skies and water, where it was possible to live from one day to the next without seeing another human being, our numbers must have looked like an army on the march.

The villages were different. At least they couldn't disappear as we drew near. They occupied the few islands of ground that rose above the level of the water, and though some could only be reached by boat, most were connected by a spider's web of narrow roadways that wound through the reeds. The people were quiet and suspicious of us at first, but when they realised we weren't going to kill or steal, they were friendly enough.

They were more in awe of Ara and her ravens than anyone else, even when they'd been told that Father was a king. And I noticed that it was our old nurse they spoke to first, calling her Wise One and bobbing their heads to her.

After a few days we came to a village that was bigger than most. It stood on a low island of dry land that rose out of the surrounding marshes. But the houses spilled over the edges of the dry area, and some of them stood out on the water itself on long poles that raised them above the mud and reed beds like the legs of herons.

As we approached the first houses, it was obvious that the people had known for some time that we were coming. The streets were full of small, dark men and women and all of them had some weapon to hand: short hunting bows, fishing spears and gutting knives that were used for cleaning the catch of the day, but which I guessed would be equally useful against people.

They parted to let us through as we rode towards what we guessed would be the centre of the village and then closed behind us and followed.

When we reached the centre an old woman was waiting for us, sitting under a huge willow tree, the only green growing thing that wasn't a reed for as far as the eye could see.

We walked the horses slowly forward and then stopped a few paces away from where the woman sat. For a moment there was silence and she stared at my father. Then Cerdic, obviously feeling that she was showing a lack of respect, suddenly barked, "Bow down before your king and queen, old woman!"

She turned her head to look at the soldier. "I'm sitting, which makes bowing difficult, but I give them their due even if you can't see it."

Father raised a calming hand at Cerdic and then nodded at the woman. "We've come to ask for your help ... "

"Against the Danes who've burned your towns and killed your soldiers, I know," said the old woman, reminding me strongly of Ara. "What can we do with our fishing spears and the slingshots we use on birds?"

"More than you know," Father answered with equal bluntness. "Your hunters and fishermen can keep watch on the enemy's movements and stop them coming into the marsh, and they can also bring information to me."

"And where will they find you, Alfred of Wessex?"

"At Athelney, deep in the reed beds."

"We know it, and we also know the safe ways to it," the old woman said. "You'll want guides and supplies."

"Yes, both," Father agreed. "And if your people find any loyal Saxon fighters hiding in the marshes, send them to me. It's time to start rebuilding the army."

"And how will you pay for all of this when the Danes have your gold, and live in your towns, and eat the flesh of your beasts and the grain of your land?"

Cerdic leapt from his horse and I think he would have done something that would have ended any hope we had of help from the marsh people. But Ara placed her hand on his shoulder as he passed her. It rested gently in the place just above where a bronze pin secured his cloak, but he spun round as though he'd been struck by a Danish war hammer.

"Peace, Cerdic Guthweinson, and listen to what our allies and your king have to say," Ara said with quiet force, then she nodded at the elder of the village. The woman returned her nod and the air seemed almost to crackle as though an unsaid greeting had passed between the two old women. It was then that I suddenly realised they were so similar in their language and looks they might have been sisters, though they obviously weren't related. Then I remembered Ara telling us long ago that the marshlands were a stronghold of the old religion. That was the link between the two ... that and the fact that they both had the power of the wise woman.

Father then went on as though nothing had happened. "When the Danes have been driven out and smashed in battle and I sit on my throne again, I will not forget the people of the marshes."

The old woman raised her head and held my father's gaze. "You would have had our help anyway, Alfred of Wessex, but when the wealth of kings is yours once again, we'll be happy to be remembered."

Edward leant across from where he sat on Cerdic's horse and whispered, "Why do they have to talk like they're living in a poem?"

I shrugged and whispered back, "They're grown-ups – it's what they do, especially when they're talking about important stuff that everyone knows'll be remembered."

"Well that's great, but I'm hungry. D'you think they'll feed us soon?"

"Hope so. But who knows?"

"Wonderful!" said Edward miserably.

Not long after that the talking ended and we were taken to a longhouse where we were given some food. I glanced secretly at Cerdic, and noticed that he carried his arm where Ara had grabbed him with care. I winced at the thought of the bruise he probably had. Our old nurse had always had power, but since Chippenham and Wessex had fallen to the Danes it was almost as though she'd decided to reveal her true nature.

I must admit I'd been surprised by how hot-headed Cerdic had been with the woman elder. Usually he was cool and careful in everything he did, but I suppose even the most experienced campaigner and soldier can make mistakes.

III

We stayed the night in the village, and the next morning we set out with a party of five guides who'd also use their hunting skills to keep us supplied during the journey.

The woman elder promised Father that she'd send out her people to look for any Saxon fighters that might be hiding in the reed beds and also to watch the enemy and keep them from entering the marshlands. The Danes might have the mightiest army that had walked the land since the time of the Romans, but in the wetlands the marsh people ruled and, if necessary, their spears and arrows would hunt Norsemen rather than birds and fish.

Within two days we reached a small settlement hidden in the deep reed beds, called Lyng. I don't think any of us could have found the place without the guides; we'd travelled over what they called 'safe causeways' and along tracks that only they were able to see. To the rest of us it seemed we were walking along ways that had been trampled moments before by otters or water voles. Once we even had to swim the horses across a wide stretch of stagnant water. But at last we spied the first huts of the village and the guides led us in.

By this point Father claimed he knew exactly where he was, but I'm not so sure. He hadn't been to Athelney since he was a boy and one reed bed and muddy village looked much the same as all the rest. Even so he said it with such confidence everyone believed him. This was something that I decided to remember. It seems that leadership is often just a matter of confidence. If you look and act as if you know what you're doing, then people will believe that you do.

We stayed less than half a day in Lyng, during which time Father and Mother met the elders. Then at last we set off on the final stage of the journey to Athelney. But in fact you could hardly call it a stage, because within less time than it used to take me to get out of bed and get dressed (when I had such a thing as a bed), we arrived at a set of embankments and earthworks that rose out of the surrounding marshes. These defended the beginning of a solid causeway that led to the island that would be our fortress and haven for the next few months.

"Looks like another marsh frog's hovel to me," said Edward when we'd all dismounted and gathered together in front of the gateway in the embankments.

"Well if it means we can stop tramping through all this mud for a while, then I'm happy to be a marsh frog," I answered.

Aethelgifu walked up to join us. "Everything and everywhere is part of God's creation, from the poorest hovel to the richest palace," she said piously.

"Well I've had enough of the 'poorest hovel' bit," said Edward. "How about putting in a good prayer for us, Aethelgifu, and getting us back into one of the 'richest palaces'? It doesn't have to be particularly big, just dry and warm, and full of stuff like good food and comfy beds ... oh, and servants to bring me whatever I want whenever I want it."

"I've already told you, I believe all of this has been sent by God to test our faith. I think it'll be a long time before any of us set foot inside a palace ... in fact, we may never live that sort of life again."

"Wonderful," said Edward moodily. "Hasn't God got anything better to do other than making our lives a misery – you know, like running the universe or something?"

Aethelgifu managed to look down her nose at him snootily, even though she was at least a head shorter. "We will receive our reward in heaven," she said with dignity.

"Well I agree with Edward," I said, making my brother look at me in surprise.

"You do?" he said suspiciously, remembering our usual rivalry. "Why?"

"Because I think God has tested us enough. And as for rewards in heaven, I wouldn't mind having some of the rewards here and now on earth, just to make things a bit easier."

"We cannot make demands of God," Aethelgifu replied sternly. "Only He knows the outcome of any divine plan."

Before the discussion could go any further, the adults called us together to stand before the earthworks that defended the causeway to Athelney. Despite the fact that I'd always thought both Father and Mother disapproved of Ara's *scinncraeft*, or magic, they both seemed quite happy now as our old nurse obviously got herself ready to carry out a ceremony of some sort.

Both her ravens were with her. They sat on her shoulders, their eyes like midnight and their feathers gleaming darkly in the bright sunlight.

We made quite an impressive company once everyone was gathered together. In the short time since the marsh people had been actively looking for Saxon fighters who'd taken refuge from the Danes in the reed beds, our numbers had increased to over fifty – and more than thirty of those were trained housecarles.

Ara raised her hands above her head and the ravens leapt into flight where they circled tightly around us, their harsh voices echoing over the silence of the wetlands. The fierce winter weather hadn't gained such a strong hold on the marshes as it had on Wessex, but as our old nurse and wise woman began to call in a loud, deep voice that mingled perfectly with the cries of her ravens, a freezing-cold wind started to blow, as though answering the strange words.

None of us understood the incantations that rose up into the air with the same sort of winged power as the dark birds that circled above us. But, as more and more words poured out, clouds began to gather on the horizon and then race over the sky towards us, driven by the icy wind.

Soon the cold blue of the heavens was swallowed up by the clouds and a shadow settled over the wetlands. The wind blew more and more strongly, making the reeds hiss like an army of snakes, and mingled with it were voices, faint and fierce and somehow not quite human. They sounded like someone had taught the feelings of hatred and anger and fear to speak, and what they said had nothing to do with calm and happy things.

Ara's ragged cloak and grey hair streamed in the icy wind, making her look as though she was flying, and her eyes stared unblinkingly as the incantation continued to pour out of her mouth.

Then suddenly her voice became less deep and we could understand the words she used as she turned to my father. Ara waited while my mother took his hand and led him to stand before her. Obviously my mother had a part to play in the strange ceremony and was giving her consent to whatever was about to happen.

"Behold the king wed to this land in the ancient rite I now perform," Ara called loudly. And as we watched she scooped mud from the causeway and smeared it on my father's forehead just as I'm told the Christian priests smear holy oil on the king during their coronation ceremonies. Then Ara placed mud on the palms of his hands and folded his fingers over it, and even smeared mud from her own fingers in his mouth. The amazing thing was that Father didn't spit it out, but stood quietly as our wise woman continued to anoint him with mud.

When she was done Ara raised her arms again. Ranhald and Raarken settled back on her shoulders and stood blinking their shining black eyes as their mistress began to speak again.

"Behold your king, beloved of the gods and now consort of the land. The rite is performed; the contract is sealed." She turned to the earthworks that stood before the causeway that led to Athelney.

"And behold his fortress from where he will lead his army in revenge on those who have defiled this kingdom!"

Then once more her voice fell into tones far deeper than normal as she chanted:

"No enemy may find this place;
we hide it in mist and shadow.
No sword may pierce this place;
we shield it with fear and power.
No army may march on this place;
we defend it with iron and blood."

Ara drew a dagger from somewhere in the black rags that billowed around her, and stabbed its razor-sharp point into the flesh of her forearm. She held the wound over the land at her feet, and after several large drops had splashed heavily into the mud, she drove the dagger into the edge of the path where earth met the water of the marshes.

At this, the icy wind suddenly dropped and, into the silence, snow began to fall.

"It is done," Ara said in a quiet voice.

The island of Athelney rose from the surrounding marshlands like a green fortress. Its shores were defended by a palisade, or high wooden wall, and its gates were protected by earthworks, just like the entrance to the causeway that led to it.

In the very centre of the space, on the highest ground, stood a royal hall that we immediately called the 'Little Palace', and with it were the other buildings that support such a place, such as the kitchens, storehouses and even a blacksmith's forge. These were structures of the old hunting lodge that had been used by my family for generations. They were much smaller than the palace buildings we were used to, in fact they were little more than a large house, and they needed a lot of cleaning and repairing to make them fit to live in, but they were the closest we'd come to a home since we'd been driven out of Chippenham.

This was my mother's domain and she immediately marshalled the few chamberlains and servants that were to be found amongst those who'd fled the Danes. My father may have been in charge of rebuilding the army and defending the land, but in effect my mother was the commander who ensured the smooth running of the entire fortress island, which was all that remained of free Wessex. And she wielded her power with a cold precision.

Our time in Athelney was spent in preparation. The marsh people led more and more fighters to our fortress and soon temporary shelters surrounded the Little Palace on top of its hill. Cerdic Guthweinson was soon busy retraining soldiers, whose numbers were small but growing by the day.

We children were allowed the freedom of the entire island of Athelney and also the surrounding wetlands. We spent hours investigating the mysterious routes and ways through the marshes, gaining a knowledge of our new home that one day might be useful. I think Father thought it was 'character building' that we learn independence by exploring in this way. Besides, we knew that Ara kept her eye on us at all times whether we could see her or not, and the marsh people also quietly made sure we didn't get lost or into difficulties of any sort.

One day Edward, Aethelgifu and I decided to explore the pools and winding causeways that led south into the deepest and most isolated parts of the wetlands. We didn't intend to go far, but as often happened we were drawn deeper and deeper into the strange watery wilderness that had become our home and refuge. But it wasn't until we noticed that the sun was beyond the point of midday that we realised how long we'd been away from Athelney.

"We'd better turn back now," Aethelgifu said. "We don't want to be making our way home in the dark."

"The sun doesn't go down for hours yet," Edward said. "But perhaps you're right – we might miss supper if we don't go back soon."

"Let's just go a bit further," I put in. "I want to see where this path leads."

"I can tell you exactly where it leads," said Edward with a snort. "To reeds and water and marshland, and then on to other paths that'll lead us to even more reeds and water and marshland."

"No, there's something else ..." I shuddered as though something strange was about to happen and looked around expecting to see Ara and her ravens, but we were still alone. "Just a bit further, and then we'll go back."

Eventually Edward and Aethelgifu agreed and we went on. It was surprisingly warm amongst the reed beds considering that it was still only January, so at least we didn't have to worry about getting cold and catching the horrible marsh fevers Ara was always warning us about.

Surprisingly Aethelgifu seemed happier than Edward about going further and spent her time pointing out the many different birds that waded through the pools on long spindly legs or scurried up and down the reeds like mice. "Look at the wealth of the world," she said happily. "Every creature knitted and stitched, every wing embroidered and embellished by the Lord himself."

"Yeah? Well don't forget, if he knitted and stitched the pretty birdies, he must also have knitted and stitched the snakes, marsh fevers and the leeches that live in the pools," Edward pointed out.

"Yes, he must," Aethelgifu replied simply.

By this time we'd travelled as far as I thought we should go and I was just about to say we should go back to Athelney when the almost constant moaning of the wind through the reeds dropped to a stillness.

"Listen! Did you hear that?" I hissed.

"Hear what? It's just gone totally quiet!" Edward snapped.

"There," I said. "A whimpering."

We all stood with our faces screwed up in concentration.

"No. Not a thing," my brother insisted.

"Yes! I heard it," said Aethelgifu. "A whimper."

"It's probably just a bird."

"Over there," I said, pointing as the sound came again.

I scrambled over to where a particularly thick stand of reeds crowded up to the path. Quickly I knelt, parted the tough stems and peered down into the clump. And there, nestled amongst the reeds, was a tiny and very muddy puppy.

Quickly I picked him up and he whimpered again.

"What's that?" Edward asked, peering closely.

"Well obviously it's a puppy," Aethelgifu answered.

"I don't think it's obvious at all. It looks like a piece of dung with legs."

I cuddled the puppy close, despite all the mud, and he raised a tiny blunt snout and licked me.

"If it is a dog it must be the runt of some huntsman's litter left out here to die," Edward went on. "Leave it where it is ... or drown it."

I glared at him. "I'll do no such thing! He's probably a refugee running from the Danes just like us ... He must have got separated from his people."

"Don't be ridiculous! Anyone running from the Danes wouldn't bother to bring a useless scrap like that along. He'd be dead weight. Throw him in the marsh."

I knew Edward was just trying to be as tough as he imagined Father's housecarles to be, but I wasn't going to let him bully me into leaving the puppy behind. "I was meant to find him. When he grows up he'll be a war-dog and fight by my side in battle."

As the words left my mouth the quiet of the surrounding marshlands deepened to almost total silence and then suddenly it was torn aside as a huge wind howled out of the sky and blasted over the reed beds.

Edward looked around nervously, but Aethelgifu moved to stand beside me. "He's a creature of God, just like we all are. He's coming home with us."

I smiled at my sister and said, "I'll call him 'Wolf.'"

But Edward laughed in an effort to shake off the strangeness of the moment. "*Wolf!* That thing? 'Mouse' would be better."

That seemed to settle everything and we set off for home without any more delay or discussion. I knew that my brother could well be right and the puppy might not ever grow into the war-dog I for some reason imagined him to be, but as I walked along I couldn't help noticing his enormous paws as he cuddled down to sleep in my arms. One day I hoped that he'd grow to fit them.

When we got back to Athelney nobody took any notice of the small scrap of muddy dog I was carrying. So it was easy to sneak into one of the sheds and wash him before Mother and Father saw him. Aethelgifu helped me while Edward watched and made unhelpful comments.

"Don't scrub too hard; you might wash him away."

"If only the same could be said about you," I answered, but then concentrated on getting the puppy clean.

At last it was done and as I dried him I realised a sturdy little dog had emerged from all the mud. He was a light fawn colour with a brown face and ears and a short, stubby tail. His muzzle was quite short but broad and when he suddenly yapped at us in happy excitement I could see he had a fine set of tiny, needle-sharp teeth.

"You should call him Moses," Aethelgifu said as she watched the little creature sniffing at all the interesting scents in his new surroundings.

"Why?"

"Because you found him in the reeds, of course. Just like Pharaoh's daughter found the original Moses."

"No, he's already been named," said Edward trying to provoke me. "Mouse. Just right for a tiny runt like him."

I looked at my brother, ready to be irritated by him as usual. He obviously hoped to spend a happy time arguing with me about the name, but I decided then and there to disarm him.

"Mouse it is then," I said and stooped down to the little animal. "Mouse," I called and held out my hand. He immediately ran to me and I scooped him up to cuddle him.

I wasn't too worried about how my parents would react to Mouse. Father often used to be surrounded by hounds when he'd been at home in any of his palaces and Mother had been brought up in the Royal Court of Mercia which, judging by some of the stories she told about her childhood, was almost stuffed with dogs. To them owning hounds was a perfectly natural situation. If anything, Athelney was unusual in having so few dogs running about.

Ara was a different matter. I could never guess how she'd react to anything, but I was soon to find out. As I carried Mouse up to the Little Palace on that first morning I found him, she suddenly fell into step beside me as though she'd just walked into the world from some other place of shadows.

"You've found your companion then," she said.

I hugged the puppy close. "Yes," I answered, and then added fiercely, "and I won't let him be taken from me!"

"I'm glad to hear it," she answered. "It's never a good idea to reject a gift."

"A gift? From whom? I found him in the marshlands."

"I'm sure you did," she answered mysteriously and Ranheld and Raarken cackled from their perch on her shoulders.

"What are you saying?" I asked, getting almost as annoyed with the wise woman as I did with Edward.

She turned her black eyes on me. "Only that some things that are lost are meant to be found. And though they may be as small and as unimportant as a puppy, they make something or some*one* complete – so that they're able to achieve important things."

"What?" I snapped, completely confused by her words. "Who and what are you talking about?"

"Important things that the unimportant help to bring about."

I gave up. When Ara wanted to be mysterious no amount of questioning would make her explain herself clearly. "Fine!" I said dismissively. "If you don't mind, I have to find some food for a hungry puppy."

Ara bowed her head graciously and I watched as she began to walk away. "Will he be a war-dog?" I suddenly called after her.

"Will his mistress be a shield maiden?" she answered without turning back.

"His mistress *is* a shield maiden!"

"Then you have your answer, Aethelflaed Cerdinga."

During this time we learnt that the Danes had started a campaign in Devon, extending their power over the west and isolating Wessex. King Guthrum had stolen the crown of my father's kingdom, but in Devon the Danish army was led by Ubba and it was he who had the legendary Raven banner. This was a war standard that was carried at the head of the Danish army and was said to be magical. It was woven by three Danish princesses who had chanted spells as they worked, making any fighting force that carried it invincible.

It seemed to us that the world was on fire. Cities and kingdoms were falling and the Danes were running wild throughout the lands. On Father's orders our own war training continued too. Even little Aethelfryth was given a tiny shield and wooden sword and learnt to use them along with the rest of us. On the surface I think Father wanted us to believe we could defend ourselves if the Danes ever attacked Athelney, but underneath I think it was more than that: we were children of the Royal House of Cerdinga and in our veins ran the blood of the ancestors who first came to the land that had been our home for generations. It was the blood of warriors and somewhere mingled deep within it was the blood of the old gods our people had worshipped for centuries before Christ came and swept aside all others. This was the beginning of our power and right to rule: this was what made us Cerdinga.

In Athelney we lived again as our ancestors had lived before us. The fine clothes and jewellery were gone; we wore whatever could be traded from the marsh people. The rich food and fancy dishes were a thing of the past too; we ate what could be hunted and gathered from the land around. And at night, we all slept as a family under the roof of the hall that had become Father's palace, along that is with some of the more important fighters and thegns who were the last representatives of the ruling class of Wessex.

We children had our own corner of the great hall where we rolled out our blankets every night and slept under the raven eye of Ara. The fact that we slept under the *real* raven eye of Raarken too made it doubly difficult to discuss the day until he finally put his head under his wing and slept. But that never happened until he'd called to Ranhald, who was too wild to come into the hall but perched on the roof outside, and answered his cawing at the close of every day. Raarken also only slept when Ara finally did, so when at last he closed his flinty eyes we knew it was safe to speak without the risk of our nurse and wise woman's hard hands slapping us into what she thought was the right state of mind for sleep.

"I heard Cerdic say that they're ready and that they're going tomorrow," Edward suddenly whispered from the near dark that was lit only by the glowing embers of the fire in the central hearth.

"Yes, I know. All the fighters are talking about it," I said as I settled Mouse on to his blankets next to my sleeping place. I'd been making sure he ate well and he was already growing so quickly that I'd had to find more blankets to make him a bigger bed.

"Who's ready for what?" Aethelgifu asked irritably. "You two always talk in riddles!"

"The raiding parties are ready," Edward explained. "The marsh people have kept the Danes out of the wetlands, but Cerdic and Father are going to lead a raid against one of their strongpoints."

"You still haven't said when," Aethelgifu pointed out, obviously more than a little annoyed that Edward and I knew about the raid and she didn't.

"Tomorrow morning. The moon's dark for the next few days so even if it's a clear night, when they reach their target there'll only be starlight."

"Which strongpoint are they going for?" she asked, surprising me that she wanted to know in such detail. Normally all her thoughts were taken up by the Church and its doings.

"It's a post that guards the main way from Somerset into Wessex. Father and Cerdic want to remind the Danes we're still undefeated," Edward told her.

"I asked Father if I could go with him on his first raid," I said importantly, wanting to remind Edward that I knew stuff too and that I was the eldest and just as much a warrior-in-training as him.

"What did he say?" he asked, his voice pleasingly edged with a sort of jealous panic.

After enjoying my small victory for a few moments I put him out of his misery and said, "He didn't say much at all ... just that I wasn't ready yet and that he'd be too distracted worrying about me if I went along. He said it was important that the first raid was a success for the sake of the men's morale."

"Oh," said Edward, all his relief summed up in that one word.

"Well I shall *pray* for our victory," said Aethelgifu. "Not all of us want to go into battle with sword and shield; some of us are the peaceful warriors of the Lord of Hosts."

"That's fine," I said, stroking Mouse who could sense the tension in the air and padded backwards and forwards between us seeking reassurance. "Every army needs holy men and women praying for it."

"Yeah," Edward agreed. "But I've heard Cerdic say that the holy ones of the Danish army are some of their best warriors. The priests of Thor carry war hammers like the god they worship and once they get into one of their holy frenzies they're almost impossible to stop."

"Bare-sarkers," I said, wanting to show that I knew about the mad fighters of the Danes as well. "But it's not only the priests that go bare-sark: any of their warriors can do it."

"Devil worshippers that allow themselves to be possessed by fighting demons," said Aethelgifu with contempt. "No right-thinking Christian would do such a thing."

"Well whatever they are, Cerdic says they're a force that's difficult to face," said Edward.

"And anyway, if you listen to the singers in the hall at night, you'll hear plenty of stories about

Saxon warriors who were bare-sarkers," I pointed out as I wrapped my fingers gently around Mouse's muzzle to stop him adding his sharp little barks to the conversation.

"Yes, but only from a time before we were shown the true path and abandoned the sinful worship of the old gods," Aethelgifu said forcefully.

Mouse stood up and suddenly started to wag his tail as though greeting someone. "Those old gods led our people for generations from long before the time we came to these islands," said a harsh voice from the shadows. "And not everyone has shown disloyalty and replaced them with this Christ from the lands of the east."

"Oh, Ara!" said Aethelgifu nervously. "We didn't know you were still awake."

"Obviously not. But even 'peaceful warriors of the Lord of Hosts' need to sleep if they want to be awake enough to grovel before their god in the morning." A shadow darker than the surrounding gloom then rose up to loom over us. "Now go to sleep, before my hand finds a reason to smack a few heads!"

Raarken added his voice as though in support of his mistress, and his flinty eyes dully reflected the embers glowing in the central hearth. It was at such times that I could almost find myself feeling sorry for King Guthrum and his Danish army. How could he hope to win when something like Ara stood against him?

IV

The next day we woke up to the noise and clamour of an army getting ready to march. The fact that it was only made up of thirty lightly armed men wasn't important. Wessex was about to strike back against the invading Danes!

I leapt up out of my blankets and ran outside with Edward close behind me, and Mouse tumbling along in our wake. The camp that surrounded the Little Palace was loud with preparations. We now had three blacksmith's forges altogether – the two new ones had been added to serve the needs of our growing army – and all of them were hard at work belching smoke and filling the air with the sharp scent of hot metal and the ringing clatter of new blades beaten on anvils.

Mouse added his little yapping voice to the clamour and then surprised himself when a much deeper bark suddenly burst out of his throat.

"This is it!" I said excitedly to Edward. "This is the moment when we begin to fight back!"

He nodded. "*I wish, I wish, I wish* I was going with them," he said, hopping from foot to foot and echoing my thoughts exactly – though I'd never admit to him that we shared anything, not even thoughts.

"We should think of the warriors who will soon be dying because of this action," Aethelgifu said piously as she walked up to join us.

Edward glanced at her sharply. "If anyone dies it's the fault of the Danes, and anyway, doesn't the Church say we have the right to defend ourselves, especially against pagans?"

"It does," she agreed. "But we should also feel sorry that those who die outside the teachings of the Church will go straight to hell."

"Difficult to worry about that when your enemy has killed your people, burned your home and driven you into exile," I said bitterly.

"Yes it is difficult, but as Christians we should try."

I fell silent for a moment with bowed head. "There, I've tried. Christian duty done."

Aethelgifu glared for a moment but said nothing. We turned back to watch the small force that had gathered on the sweep of open land where Cerdic and his hand-picked group of warriors carried out most of the weapons-training and mock battles needed to prepare our fighters for the coming war. Men and also some women who wanted to strike back at the Danes had been trickling into Athelney in a non-stop flow almost from the first day we'd arrived. The marsh people had been true to their word and continued to guide Saxon fighters to our stronghold, as well as defending the borders of the wetlands from the enemy.

Some of the people they brought to us were trained soldiers who helped Cerdic and the others with the preparations, but most were raw and untested and were put through a tough training regime where the unfit and unsuitable were weeded out. Of those that were left, a quarter of their number now stood ready to go on the first proper strike against the Viking army since Chippenham had fallen. The rest would be left behind to defend Athelney against possible counter-attack.

As we watched, a clamour rose up as two tough-looking warriors strode out of the Little Palace and joined the force. It took me a moment to realise that the soldier walking with Cerdic was my father. I'd seen him often enough in battle gear, so it wasn't his clothing and weaponry that confused me; it was more than that.

Edward summed it up perfectly when he leant in close and almost whispered, "He looks just like a warrior-king from the old stories!"

"Yes! That's it," I agreed. "He's not just our father now, he's ..." I searched for the words. "He's ..."

"He's *Wessex* itself. He's the kingdom and the land," a voice suddenly said behind us, and we both spun round to see Ara standing quietly watching the muster of the small fighting force. Mouse stood and wagged his tail in greeting and when Raarken and Ranheld leant forward from Ara's shoulders to stare at him, he dropped his head on to his forepaws, raised his rump and wagged his tail in the air, inviting them to play.

"You're seeing the mystery of kingship," Ara went on. "He's not just a man who wears a crown on his head; he's wedded to the land itself. In the old days, when the people followed the gods of our ancestors, they understood. The king was like the consort, the husband of the earth goddess who was the very land beneath their feet. It was his duty to protect that land, to fight for her and even die for her if needed."

We nodded as though we understood and turned back to watch as Father greeted his warriors. They cheered and beat their axes and swords on the light wicker shields they carried. It all felt like we weren't actually a part of what we were seeing. It was almost as though we were being allowed to witness a ritual and ceremony that we weren't yet ready to take part in.

The soldiers then formed ranks and prepared to march out, but before they could move, a figure stepped through the main doorway of the Little Palace and stood quietly watching. It was my mother, but instead of wearing the old workaday homespun we'd got used to seeing her in since we'd arrived in Athelney, she was wearing the beautiful dress she'd had on when we ran from Chippenham. Somehow the stains and the rips and rents had been repaired and the fabric cleaned and she looked like a Saxon queen again.

Father turned to face her, and then raised the double-headed axe he was holding in salute. My mother bowed her head slightly and smiled, then the army marched away, singing as they went.

Mother turned to go back into the palace, but paused when she saw us. I realised that she was now in sole command of the defence of Athelney, and I looked at her closely, aware of a sense of power that seemed to radiate from her like heat, the same sense of power that seemed to surround Ara. It was then that I saw the strangest thing of the entire morning. Our old nurse curtsied to the ground and both Raarken and Ranhald, who'd been sitting on her shoulders, rose up into the air cawing.

We fell to our knees as though something had forced us down, and we found ourselves staring at the ground. When eventually we looked up, Mother had gone inside.

"I'm going to pray for the army," Aethelgifu said suddenly. I'd forgotten all about my sister in the excitement of the force's departure. "I'm sure the Lord of Hosts will grant victory to the righteous."

We watched as she hurried away, clutching the cross she wore round her neck as though she needed something to hang on to.

We heard nothing for two days. The soldiers who'd been left behind to defend Athelney increased their training times, and some were sent with the marsh people to patrol the reed beds. But otherwise everyone tried to carry on with the normal routine that'd been established over the time we'd been in the marshes.

Edward and I spent more time training, trying to outdo each other in fighting skill and strength. We both tried to carry full-sized shields, but had to admit we weren't yet strong enough, and used instead the lighter wicker shields that were only half the weight. We'd been promised that when we could carry the full-sized equipment every soldier used in a proper battle, we could go on patrol along the borders of the marshlands. But that was some way off yet.

One damp, drizzly afternoon after weapon training, I sat staring at the glowing embers in the central hearth of the great hall. I had my arm around

Mouse's shoulders and realised that he was getting broader as he put on weight and muscle.

"Watching fire-pictures?" a voice asked, making me jump. It was Ara, who had done her usual trick of walking up quietly behind me. I sometimes thought that her ability to move about without making a sound was how she knew so much about what was going on. But I was about to find out that I was wrong.

"I'm no seer," I answered at last, naming those with the gift to see the future in the fire. "Otherwise I'd try and see how the raiding party is doing and whether Father is safe and well. But all I can see is burning wood."

Ara nodded for a moment and said, "Come with me." Then turned and walked from the hall.

I climbed to my feet and followed with Mouse. Soon we'd passed through the village of tents that had grown up around the Little Palace and we headed for the main gate that opened out on to the causeway. I hadn't actually left the island of Athelney for some time, so it felt odd passing through the palisaded defences and out into the world of reeds and deep waters.

Just as I set foot on the causeway, a curlew flew over calling, the wild loneliness of its cry echoing over the wide skies and seeming to announce my presence, as though I was someone important.

Ara led the way to where a punt, one of the flat-bottomed boats the marsh people used, was tied to a post that had been driven into the firmer ground at the edge of the causeway. She climbed in first and then stood and watched, arms folded, as I picked up Mouse with some difficulty and scrambled after.

Then just as she picked up the pole that is used to drive the boat along, Ranhald and Raarken descended from the sky in a beating and clattering of wings. They took up their usual post on Ara's shoulders, and called raucously as their mistress took us out over the black waters of the marshlands.

Mouse hung his head over the side and tried to bite the water as it slid past.

"Where are we going?" I asked after we'd been gliding through the reed beds for some time.

"To the Black Pool."

"Where's that?"

"In the marshes."

"But we're in the marshes now."

"Yes."

"Can't you be more specific then?"

"No."

"When will we get there?"

"When we arrive."

I gave up. When Ara was in one of her mysterious moods no amount of prodding and probing would make her reveal more than she wanted. Eventually we came to a wide basin of water that was lined by dead trees and darkly reflected the grey sky. We glided slowly across and when we reached the far side Ara drove the punt up on to the bank.

"This way," she said and led us along a narrow pathway that wound between stretches of open water. At last she stopped under an ancient willow that hung over a pool no bigger than the shield that used to hang above my father's throne in Chippenham.

"Now what?" I asked.

"Now sit and watch, quietly."

I sat on the small tussock of grass she pointed to, took Mouse on to my lap and waited while the old woman spread her arms wide over the water.

Slowly a murmuring rose up into the air and it took me some time to realise that it was Ara chanting to herself. Suddenly a wind sprang up, ruffling the glass-like surface of the pool. Then as suddenly it fell away again to stillness.

"Look into the water and tell me what you can see," Ara said quietly.

"Nothing but stagnant black ... no, wait! I can see ... *what* can I see? I can see an *image*, a moving picture of soldiers!"

"The raiding party," Ara informed me.

"The raiding ... !" I scrambled away from the water. "This is *scinncraeft*; this is magic! The Church says magic is evil."

"*Scinncraeft* is merely a tool that can be used for good or bad," Ara answered, and then stood in silence while she obviously considered her words. "Would you say a hammer is evil? Would you say a knife is evil? No," she eventually went on. "But undoubtedly they can be used to do evil things, in just the same way that they can be used for good. I could stab you with a knife, or I could use it to make you a meal when you're hungry."

"I'm not hungry," I answered stubbornly and then watched as Ara's expression changed from amusement to anger and then back again.

"Think your own thoughts, Aethelflaed, not those the Church tells you to think! In the coming years the fight against the Danes will be long and vicious; do you think that the Church will be able to tell you what to do? Will you act only in the way the Church tells you to act? You live in a fierce world, Daughter of Kings, and to survive in it you must be equally fierce. You must also be much cleverer than your enemies!"

Ranhald and Raarken suddenly leant forward on her shoulders and croaked loud and long as though adding their own opinions to the debate.

"Now, will you look into the pool and see what fate has been woven for your father and the raiding party, or will you refuse and be kept safe by the teachings of the Church, just as the Church kept Chippenham safe when Guthrum and his Danes came knocking on the gates?"

I sat in silence for a few moments and then I took a deep breath and leant out over the black waters of the pool. Ara nodded, an expression on her face that was as close to a smile as she ever achieved.

"What do you see?" she asked.

"Just black water ... no, wait – the image is making itself again ..." I watched as shape and form emerged from the shadows and shimmer of the pool.

Even light was somehow made from the darkness and I watched as Father, Cerdic and their soldiers followed a narrow path that wound through the tall reeds of the marshes under a sky of crowding stars.

The picture was so real I felt that I could reach out and touch them, but I seemed to be watching from a place above them, like a low-flying bird. Mouse watched with me, and when he saw our people he barked once and then fell silent. Now I saw the soldiers reach a place where the reed beds suddenly stopped as a wide road sliced through them, as sharp as a knife cut. This I knew was the old Roman road that led to the south and eventually to Chippenham.

The image showed me a raised square of land that stood adjoining the road surface. It was protected by banks of earth and on the top of these I could see men standing guard. The raised square was obviously the remains of an old Roman strongpoint that had protected the important route. But the legionaries were long gone, and the guards I could see were Danes trying to defend the lands they'd invaded.

As I watched I saw the reeds lining the road swaying in a sudden breeze – and then amazingly I felt it stir my hair, almost as though I was actually standing with my father hidden in the mud of the marshes.

My view changed and I realised the raiding party was working its way down towards the strongpoint under the covering hiss and whisper of the wind-blown reeds.

I held my breath and watched as my father drew his sword, an action that was echoed by all his soldiers. Slowly they crept nearer and suddenly a heron leapt into startled flight, drawing the attention of the enemy. The Saxons sank down into the reeds as the enemy levelled their spears and glared out over the land. I felt my heart hammering in my chest. But after a few tense moments, the Danes relaxed again, leaning on their spears and chatting amongst themselves like old women in the marketplace.

"WESSEX! FOR WESSEX!" my father suddenly yelled, leaping to his feet, his voice echoing over the quiet of the marshes. His men answered as one: "FOR WESSEX!" and they erupted from the reeds in a disciplined rush and stormed the strongpoint. The guards sent up a warning shout and soon Danes began to pour out of the low shelters that stood in the shadows of the embankment.

"Hit them! Hit them now!" my father roared. "Don't let them raise the shield wall!"

Our soldiers smashed into the enemy like a rockslide, knocking many to the ground and stabbing them where they lay. Even though our warriors were armed much more lightly than the Danes, the enemy fell back, scrambling away as fast as they could. But the Vikings are strong and brave fighters and they rallied around a tall, grey-bearded man.

Father ran forward, crouching low as a hunting wolf, and his men followed so that they hit the enemy like a spear-point, driving through their ranks in a controlled fury that forced the Danes back, though they still fought strongly, retreating one slow step at a time. The grey-bearded warrior kept his men steady in the face of the Saxon onslaught. Father's sword flashed and flickered like an iron lightning bolt, and then he ran forward under a hail of axes and stabbed the greybeard in the throat.

But the discipline of the Danes still held and they fought on, falling like marsh reeds before a storm wind. They tried to link shields and form a wall, but the raiding party drove at them again and again, breaking them apart. Then Father rallied his warriors into a tight wedge formation and drove forward again, and suddenly the enemy seemed to despair as they watched the mighty Saxon king leading his fighters. Without word or warning they suddenly turned and ran. Father stopped his force giving chase, and after they'd cheered themselves hoarse, he sent them to loot the enemy's camp. Before they left they set fire to the shelters and burned everything they couldn't carry away.

The vision faded and I found myself staring into the depths. Mouse stood with his nose almost touching the water and I pulled him back. A small golden birch leaf twined and twisted on some hidden current and I watched it for a while until a voice broke into my quiet:

"Now you know the raiding party has been successful."

I nodded thoughtfully as I remembered everything I'd just seen. Then I turned to look directly at Ara who stood behind me. "You know it to be true then?"

"As I know my own name."

I sat up and took a deep breath. I wasn't yet ready to believe that what I'd seen was the truth. I wasn't yet ready to shout and scream in joy and relief.

We'd been in exile for so long and the Danes seemed unbeatable. Why should I accept as true a few pictures conjured by an old woman whose closest friends were ravens?

"If you can see the future, why didn't you warn us of the attack that was going to be made on Chippenham?" I finally asked.

"I can only see what has already happened, and sometimes what is happening as I watch. I've been given a vision of the future only once before."

"Not much use then, this gift of yours."

Ranhald and Raarken cawed harshly as though in answer. "Very few can see the future and none of those can see it when they wish. The vision is given only when the gods wish it, and is never all there is to know."

I nodded, but before I could say anything more, Ara went on in an icy voice: "And a vision of what has just happened at least brings news swiftly!"

"So you can make a vision whenever you wish then?" I asked. "And make it wherever you are?"

The old woman's eyes blazed, but eventually she admitted, "No, they too only come when the gods wish it."

"So, they're useful when they bother to happen."

A silence fell that was so deep I could hear the still waters of the Black Pool shifting against the mud.

"Well the visions have bothered to happen now, and you've seen the victory your father has gained against the enemy that everyone thought was unbeatable," Ara said at last.

"But how can I know they're true?"

Just then the high and excited voice of a hunting horn suddenly blasted into the air. It was so close it obviously came from Athelney and I knew that strict orders had been given that hunting horns would only be sounded for victory.

I shouted then!

I screamed then!

Mouse joined in, leaping around me as in joy and relief I shouted and screamed and danced in the mud so that the scent of the marshes filled my head and gave a perfume to the knowledge we'd all just been given. The Danes could be beaten! The Danes could be broken! The Danes could be trodden into the dirt!

I knew now that Wessex would rise again and that the enemy would be beaten to his knees.

Ranhald and Raarken joined in the excitement and raising the manes of feathers around their heads they called long and loud into the wide sky of the wetlands.

V

The victory feast was small in comparison to the banquets we'd once had in the royal palaces of Wessex. But in our hearts it was the greatest we'd ever had. As many people as possible crammed into the small mead hall of the Little Palace and the rest spilled out into the surrounding village of tents, where tables were set up for all the food and drink.

Many of the marsh people joined us; after all this was their victory as much as ours. Without their patrols that had kept the Vikings out of the wetlands we wouldn't have been able to prepare for the coming struggle.

But by the next day, allowing for a lot of sore heads, the training and preparations went on. Wessex was still in the hands of the Danes, and they still fought in Devon too under the command of General Ubba, he who carried the magical Raven banner. Edward and I joined in with this training, working hard at building up our strength and skills. Mouse came with us, watching from the edge of the training ground and barking in excitement as the warriors clashed shields and beat at each other with blunted spears and swords. Soon he would join us and learn the commands of the war-dog. But for now he had to be content to watch as Edward and I struggled to become the warriors we so desperately wanted to be. We both instinctively knew that a decisive battle against the Danes was coming, and if at all possible we wanted to be part of it.

But Edward as a boy would always have the advantage over me. Being the only son he was likely to be elected king by the council when the time came. And because of this it was also more likely that Father would take him on patrol to gain battle experience.

One day during training, Cerdic had paired us off to practise hand-to-hand fighting. And during the sessions of sword, axe and spear practice we had time to discuss the coming fighting.

"The word is we're sending out another patrol this week," said Edward as he hacked at me and I easily sidestepped and hit him on the shoulder with my wooden practice sword.

"I've heard it's more than a patrol," I answered as Edward charged and I turned and smashed him in the back with my shield. He was already bigger and stronger than me, but I was faster and had quickly learnt the trick of using my opponent's own strength against him. Something I enjoyed as I watched my brother grovelling in the dust.

He struggled to his feet and came at me again. "More? How much more?"

"The biggest we've sent against the Danes so far, according to Cerdic," I answered, surprising myself by how easy it was to 'embroider' the rumours I'd heard.

"When did he say that, and why wasn't I told?" Edward hit my shield with all his strength, sending a shock through my arm and making me step back.

"When you weren't there, and as for telling you ..." I drove my sword through the defence of his over-reaching arm and lay the point at his throat. "It obviously just never occurred to him."

For a moment he scowled, but Edward was learning things too and he grinned at me. "You're the winner, sis." He lowered his shield and sword. "You know, we're going to have to work together if we're going to find out everything we need to know. We're better off as allies than rivals."

Mouse now joined us from where he'd been watching from the edge of the training ground. He jumped around us in excitement for a while but then sat down squarely in front of Edward, his mouth wide and laughing as he stared up into my brother's face.

Edward squatted down and rubbed Mouse's chest roughly, sending the dog into a frenzy of excitement. "You know about things, sis. Lots of things; you're clever. You see *beyond* things, you see what could be ... like Mouse here. I thought he was a runt, but you said he would be a war-dog some day and look at him now: he's growing fast and looks like he'll make a big dog when his bones finally knit. But *I'm* not stupid either and one day I think I'll make a good king, as long as the Witan votes for me, but even a good king needs friends and allies, especially clever ones. So what do you say?" He looked up at me. "Allies or rivals?"

I stood in silence as I thought over his words. Sparring with Edward was always good fun, whether we used weapons on the training grounds drawing blood and bruises or words that sparked jealousy and a bitter sense of rivalry. But perhaps it was time to take a different route. Certainly it was true that sometimes one of us found out things that the other knew nothing about, and working together could double our potential for information gathering. And he was right: when we were older and trying to make our way in the world, we'd both need allies. I looked at my brother as he watched me smiling from where he squatted with Mouse and I finally made a decision.

"I think you're right," I said at last. "We *are* better off as allies. So let's do just as you say and work together against all those who try to keep things from us. We can share everything we find out and learn as much as we can!"

Edward spat in his open palm. "Pax?" he said, using the Latin word for peace.

"Pax," I agreed as I spat in my own palm and shook his hand.

Mouse wagged his tail so hard he almost fell over and when he barked his approval it had the loud and deep tones of an adult dog. I decided that the world had better take care. Aethelflaed and Edward Cerdinga had a mighty war-dog as an ally and soon our enemies would know it.

As it turned out the rumour of a large-scale raid that I'd taunted Edward with was just that ... a rumour. Cerdic hadn't really told me anything; I'd just wanted to make Edward jealous. But all that was behind us: I and my only brother were now allies. In fact, though we didn't know it at the time, that one small agreement would last throughout our lives and would change the island of Britain forever.

The Viking army had its camp below the walls of the fortress. In the centre flew the magic Raven banner that made any army that carried it invincible. The scent of the sea rose up from the shore below the cliff where the fortress stood, and the calls of the gulls that wheeled and dived over the walls sounded eerily like the cries of frightened children on the early-morning air. The Saxon commander felt the fear of his men around him. These were only part-time soldiers of the fyrd; a long siege would have them beaten before they'd even raised a sword.

He made his decision quickly and gave the order by word of mouth: there'd be no booming horns that would warn the Vikings of their plan. The men gathered in a silent knot behind the main gate, shields settled on arms, swords and spears drawn and raised ready. They knew enough to keep close ranks even in the charge.

The gates opened and they rolled out, a solid wedge of iron and wood and steel. They ran in silence obeying the given orders. The Viking camp was quiet. Their lookouts expected nothing like this from the half-trained Saxons.

Then at last a warning shout, the war horns growled and the Vikings scrambled to raise their shields around the magic banner. Voices shouted in panic, but this time the words were Danish. The Saxons hit them like a hammer and now they gave the war cry, now they roared, now they raged their hatred of the invader. But still they kept their ranks, shield overlapping shield, spear and sword striking again and again like the fangs of an adder.

The Danish shield wall stood unbroken and unbreakable. The Saxons beat against it like a stormy sea against an immovable rock. The Raven banner rose up over the heads of the Great Army, and the Saxons drove forward in desperation to seize it. The line of shields before them tightened, bristling with spears and axes.

For a moment the Saxons drew back, paused and then smashed forward again, the crash of shield on shield, blade on blade, rising into the air and echoing over the land. The warriors stood toe to toe, their shields grinding together as they hacked and slashed at each other. The screams of the dying filled the air and the ringing clash of steel clamoured over the battle. But then, almost impossibly, the Danish line gave back a step. Encouraged, the Saxons pushed forward, their swords chopping and thrusting as they sensed the incredible. The enemy gave back another step and with a joyous roaring heave the soldiers of the fyrd rolled forward in a concerted push against the enemy line. In desperation the Danish commanders rapped out orders and the wall of shields almost straightened, but the Saxons smashed against it and, with a final roar, broke the enemy line.

The Danes were thrust aside, falling in heaps. A frantic last stand of Vikings quickly formed around *the magic Raven banner, but the Saxon fyrd drove forward, crashing through the wall of shields and wrenched the banner away. Now it rose against the dawn sky held in Saxon hands.*

The Vikings left alive turned to run, but thousands fell to the swords and spears of the chasing fyrd. Soon the enemy all lay dead or wounded and their dragon boats burned on the nearby shore. The men of the fyrd finally stopped and stood in silence, unable to believe what they'd done. The commander ripped the magic banner from its pole and then broke it over his knee.

A single cheer rose up and then in a great crash thousands of voices joined it ...

Father led many raids against the Danes. More and more Saxon fighters joined us, and soon we had a solid core of over a thousand trained soldiers who would act as the anchor and centre for any army we sent against King Guthrum, General Ubba and their invading Vikings.

Then one day when the hall of the Little Palace was filled with people eating the first meal of the day, the high-pitched call of the hunting horn rose into the air. A silence fell and I immediately looked to where

Father sat. He stood slowly, his head tilted to one side as he stared down the hall to the main doors.

Everyone followed his gaze and soon the sound of running feet could be heard drawing closer and closer. I remember it was so quiet I could hear Edward's breathing as he too stared at the doors. The hunting horns only called to announce victory.

Suddenly the doors burst open and a soldier stood silhouetted against the bright morning sunlight. For a moment his dark shape was as unmoving as a doorpost, but then he leaped into the air:

"MY LORD! MY LORD ... THE RAVEN BANNER HAS FALLEN!"

I gasped, the small sound falling into the silence that followed like a blast of wind in a winter gale.

"Where did it fall and to whom?" Father asked quietly.

"To Ealdorman Odda and the fyrd of Devon," the soldier answered, and again the following silence deepened. The fyrd were the ordinary men of the Saxon world, part-time soldiers who trained once a month and then went home to carry on with their jobs as farmers, bakers, potters or whatever other work they did. It was these men who had defeated a Viking army! Not only that, but they'd defeated a Viking army that was carrying the magical Raven banner!

The silence deepened again and I watched my father's face closely, knowing in my heart that this was the victory *he'd* wanted.

"Was King Guthrum in command?" he asked, his voice measured and steady.

"No, My Lord, their general was Ubba. It's said that he crossed into Devon to extend the Dane's control of the west."

Father nodded. "Of course; the natural thing for any invader to do. What happened?"

"Odda and his fyrd were trapped in the fortress of Countisbury," the messenger shrugged. "They broke out and attacked the Danes when they least expected it. Ubba was killed along with most of his men and the banner was taken."

Father's face was expressionless. "Then Guthrum and his army remain to be beaten."

Edward and I looked at each other, both of us caught between conflicting feelings: joy that Ubba and his men were dead, and that the Raven banner had fallen, but disappointed that after all his work, Father himself hadn't had this victory.

My mother who'd sat as silent as the rest of us during this exchange now stood and placed her hand on Father's shoulder. He seemed to wake then from his thoughts, and turning to her he suddenly threw back his head and let out a huge bark of laughter.

"We smashed them! Ubba is dead! The Raven banner has fallen!" Then throwing all royal dignity aside he leapt up on to the table, dragging my mother with him, and there they danced amongst the ale pots and platters even though there was no music to be heard but our cheers and screams of joy and relief.

The shouting and celebrations flowed outwards from the Little Palace like a river in flood and soon all of Athelney was loud with cheering and laughter. Edward, Mouse and I leapt up and followed the flow out into the compound. We were so excited we ran on through the celebrations, Mouse's bark echoing over the fortress, joining in with the dancing, and cheering ourselves hoarse with the soldiers. We lost ourselves completely in the celebrations until we arrived somehow at the gate in the defences that led out into the marshes.

It was only when Ara stepped out into our path that some of the excitement drained away from us and we realised that our nurse hadn't been with us at breakfast. In fact we hadn't seen her since late the previous night.

"Come with me," she said quietly.

It was a command rather than a request and we were so used to being told what to do by her that we fell in behind without a word and followed. She led us through the gates and along a path that wound away from the main causeway through the reed beds. I almost expected her to take us to the punt she had hidden in the reeds like she did when she showed me the Black Pool. But instead she took us along a narrow path that opened up into a small island of dry land that nestled almost immediately under the walls of Athelney's defences.

There were the remains of a fire in the centre of the space, and we stood and watched as Ara laid some dry twigs and larger sticks over the ashes. We looked at each other. Neither of us could even guess what she wanted, but we waited patiently to see what she'd do. Whatever else our old nurse was, she was never less than interesting.

This was proved almost immediately when the cold ashes spontaneously burst into flames.

Mouse let out a bark of surprise and tried to sniff the flames until I pulled him back.

"Hot embers from the last fire must've lit it," Edward muttered. I nodded but both of us knew that Ara had called the blaze with her magic.

She then stared into the sky and called out, using words that neither of us understood but which to me sounded like the land itself would sound if it had a voice.

Two black specks appeared high in the sky and gradually resolved themselves into Raarken and Ranhald as they flew closer. They descended to Ara's shoulders, their wings held stiff and curved from their sides like arms embracing the nothingness of the air. When they'd settled they looked at us with their eyes of glittering jet and croaked as though greeting us.

Edward and I stared at the strange figure of three that now stood before us, the old woman of power and her two companion ravens. The small clearing in the reeds seemed to take on the same sort of atmosphere you sometimes find in an empty church, when the fading evening light has pooled its shadows between the columns and the walls, and the only other light comes from a single candle burning over the altar. We held our breath waiting for what would come next.

"Sit down; you're making the place look untidy," Ara said, breaking the strange atmosphere that had accumulated about us.

"Where?" I asked, looking at the mud and reed debris around us.

"Isn't the ground of Mother Earth good enough for you?"

Edward shrugged at me and after finding the firmest and driest spot we sat down.

"So?" Edward prompted.

"So?" Ara echoed him.

"I suppose you brought us here for a reason," I added into the following silence.

"Can you never be still? Does there always have to be a reason for every action?"

"No, I can't sit still," I answered tartly. "And yes, there does have to be a reason for every action, and an action for every reason for that matter."

I was quite pleased with what I thought was my clever answer, but I braced myself for Ara's reply. It was almost sure to be sharp. But she surprised me by smiling instead.

"And there in that one reply we have exactly who you are, Aethelflaed Cerdinga," she said. "A maker of happenings, one with the energy to do and the intelligence to do it well."

"And what about me?" Edward asked, the old jealousy reviving.

Ara turned her dark eyes on him. "Oh, you're almost exactly the same. From the same mould of the same womb ... but with even more ruthlessness than your sister. You'll make a mighty king."

"But no woman has the power of a king," I said quietly. "There'll be no place for my making and none for my doing."

Suddenly Raarken and Ranhald called loudly, their gruff and rough voices echoing over the reed beds, the ruffs of feathers standing proud about their necks and their midnight eyes glittering.

Ara's laughter mingled strangely with their calls and she held my gaze. "No place for your making and doing, you think? You may never have the power of a king, but you will have the towering strength of a woman. Though I think they'll call you a 'Lady' when you use it."

"What do you mean?" I asked.

"Sometimes secretive things need to keep their secrets," she replied.

"Yes, but you still haven't said why you've brought us here," Edward said, diverting the course of the talk into a new direction.

"To celebrate the defeat of the Danes," Ara finally answered.

We were close enough to Athelney to hear that the singing and the joyful shouting was still going on and then looked at the mud and emptiness around us.

"To celebrate?" said Edward questioningly.

"Yes," Ara replied simply, then added, "When magic power is broken sometimes the victor needs to be acknowledged ... if only quietly."

I was getting annoyed with the old woman's mysteriousness by this point and snapped, "Look, if you've something to say, just say it!"

Ara nodded. "Then I will. It takes the power of ravens to break the power of Raven banners. And perhaps it should be acknowledged that Saxon *scinncraeft* is sometimes stronger than Danish *scinncraeft*."

A deep silence fell and we stared at the old woman and her huge black birds.

"You mean—"

"And perhaps one day soon it'll be said that Saxon armies are stronger than those of the Danes as well," Ara interrupted.

Edward climbed to his feet. "You mean that you and your ravens—"

"Sometimes secretive things need to keep at least some of their secrets," the old woman interrupted again.

"You broke the power of the Raven banner," I whispered, finally putting into words the thoughts in our heads.

Ara said nothing for a while then said, "Not me or my ravens ... we were but the sword in the hands of the gods."

Edward threw back his head and screamed aloud for joy. But Ara held up her hand. "Say nothing of this to anyone else. The magic works best in secret."

VI

After this things moved quickly. With the arrival of March the cold weather was loosening its grip on the land. The raids led by the king against the Danes increased until they became a daily event. More and more Saxon fighters joined us in our stronghold and regular reports came in of ealdormen in the conquered lands defying the invaders and calling out the fyrd to fight back against Guthrum and his professional fighters. All of this meant that even the most unwarlike of our people gained an experience of fighting that they'd never had before. Without meaning to, the Danish Great Army had made warriors of a peaceful people and those people were beginning to fight back!

It was now that Mouse began his training as a war-dog. He was growing quickly and I hoped that one day he'd stand as tall as Aethelfryth and have a chest as deep and round as a young pony. Cerdic Guthweinson put him and me through our paces and Mouse took to the commands easily. Soon he knew exactly when I wanted him to wait for orders, when to be silent and when to attack. And the warriors who stood against him in training had to be well padded against the power of his massive jaws.

"He'll do," Cerdic said decisively one day after a training session.

"So when can he fight?" I asked eagerly.

"When you do," he answered. "You're the mistress of this war-dog, no one else."

"And when can I fight?"

The old soldier looked at me with narrow assessing eyes. "Soon enough ... but not yet."

Then the momentous day finally came when everything was as ready as it would ever be and the call was sent out from Athelney.

For once all four of us royal children were together enjoying the early spring sunshine and idly chatting outside the main doors of the Little Palace after our daily round of weapons training. Aethelgifu had just been giving us a lecture on how we should be preparing ourselves for the coming celebration of Easter, and little Aethelfryth was playing quietly with her doll now that she'd been allowed to put aside her small wooden training sword. Mouse simply lay and snored in the sunshine, his huge feet matching his strengthening legs and fast-growing body.

"Father has promised to build an abbey and church on Athelney when he's defeated the Danes," said Aethelgifu.

"Good idea," said Edward. "When you have to fight Guthrum and his Great Army, it's best to get as many on your side as possible."

"God is the Lord of Hosts, after all," Aethelgifu went on as though she hadn't heard him. "Who better to help in time of war?"

We were all sitting on stools that we'd positioned against the sunny south-facing wall of the Little Palace and I leant back against the slowly warming wattle and daub and stretched my legs out in front of me. "Well whether or not God decides to help in return for the building of an abbey and a church, it's still going to be a hard fight."

Nobody replied to that. It was obvious the Danes were going to fight as viciously and as bravely as they always did, and no one could say how it would end. The entire fortress island of Athelney was in a state of uproar as we got ourselves as ready as we could for the coming battle.

Father became an even more distant figure we hardly ever spoke to. He was too busy to do anything other than train his army, lead raids and plan for the coming campaign against Guthrum. Sometimes he would make the effort to spend a little time with us at breakfast or just before we went to bed, but he was so distracted with all the preparations, he might as well have not been with us. And Mother was just the same. Any time she had when she wasn't ensuring that the non-military side of Athelney ran as smoothly as the well-oiled wheels on a goods wagon, she was talking with Father, their heads close together, shutting out the world, shutting out everyone including their children. But we all understood and accepted the situation, of course: we were children of the Royal House of Cerdinga. The first duty of a ruler is to rule.

I looked out now over the training grounds where two divisions of our soldiers were demonstrating their part in those very preparations by raising the shield wall and fighting against each other with blunted weapons. I immediately spotted the weakness in the left wing of one of the fighting sections.

"The left wing isn't holding its position," Edward pointed out before I could say anything. "It'll collapse any moment now."

As we watched the wall fell with a dull rattle of tumbling shields and the shouts of swearing soldiers.

Mouse woke up and woofed once at the tangle of shields and weapons.

"Boobies!" said little Aethelfryth, using her favourite insult.

"Exactly," I agreed. "And they'd be dead boobies if it was a real battle."

But before anyone said anything else a sound began to rise up and over the entire stronghold of Athelney. We stopped to listen. At first I thought it was just the wind blowing through the reed beds that surrounded the island. But then I realised it was the voice of rumour spreading through all the people of our small community. Word was passing from mouth to mouth. Something was about to happen, something momentous: something that would bring about the change we'd all been waiting for.

"What is it they're saying?" Edward asked, staring out over the crowded space below us.

"I don't know," I answered. "Let's go down and find out!"

But before we could move Father suddenly burst on to the training ground. He seemed to appear from nowhere and I found myself scanning the area for any sign of Ara and her ways with *scinncraeft*. But she was nowhere to be seen, and my attention was soon seized again by the bright spectacle of my father. He was dressed in his full battle gear and every piece of iron and steel, copper, brass and bronze had been polished to its highest brilliance. Even the leather covering of his round shield and every belt and strap had been buffed to a sheen so that he glittered and glowed like an image of Thunor himself, the old god that the Danes call Thor.

He leapt up on to a box that someone had placed in the very centre of the training ground and the murmuring and muttering fell away into total silence. It was so quiet I could clearly hear as he drew a deep breath.

"It is now," he said in a soft voice that travelled to every corner of Athelney. "The time is now, people of Wessex. The magic Raven banner has fallen, and Saxon iron has drawn Danish blood again and again. The time is now to send out the word of calling. Be it known to all men and women of the Saxons that I summon the entire free fyrd of Wessex and all Saxon lands to Saint Egbert's Stone in Wiltshire."

The silence returned and deepened to a depth that allowed the distant singing of a lark to fall into the space where my father stood and fill it to the brim. We all of us knew that we were listening to history, that we were listening to the resurgence of a nation.

As I watched, my father slowly drew his sword and held it high so that it shone in the brilliant sunshine. Then out crashed his voice at battle-pitch:

"THE CERDINGAS WILL RISE! THE SAXONS WILL RISE! WE WILL DRIVE THE DANES FROM OUR LANDS! WE WILL BREAK THEIR SHIELD WALL! WE WILL BURN THEIR SHIPS! WE SHALL WATER OUR FIELDS WITH THEIR BLOOD!"

His words rang over the land and as the last echo faded to silence a roar boomed in reply:

"THE SAXONS WILL RISE! THE SAXONS WILL RISE!"

Over the following days the call was carried to as many Saxon settlements, farms and homesteads as possible, summoning the fyrd as part of a new army whose anchor and centre would be made up of the band of my father's thousand warriors who were as experienced and well trained as the Danish Great Army itself.

The call stated that all should gather at Saint Egbert's Stone, and allowed time for equipment to be got ready and other preparations to be made. And here was something else that I learnt about leadership and rule: when you roused the people with great announcements and with huge celebrations, a need to return to the ordinary and everyday followed quickly behind. You may be making history, but to make it work properly you had to do all of the boring bits too. For every single hero preparing to sacrifice all in a cause, there are at least as many other ordinary people needed to get them to the right place at the right time so that they can be heroic.

If Ara was right and I grew to be a woman with real power to effect and change the world I lived in, then

I had to learn and remember that the great changers and reformers could only change and reform the world with the help of the small and the humble.

But I wasn't that powerful yet, and I could only stand and watch as our kingdom prepared for one of the most decisive battles it would ever face.

VII

At last the time arrived when my father and his thousand warriors were almost ready to march out to meet with the free fyrds of the Saxon lands. Our spies told us that fighters were heading for the meeting place at Saint Egbert's Stone near a settlement called Westbury in Wiltshire, but numbers were unclear because they were moving in small groups so as not to attract the attention of the Danes until they were ready to fight.

It was noon on another bright spring day and the atmosphere felt as though a storm was about to break. Which in a way I suppose it was: not a storm of lightning and rain, but of swords and spears. And when it was over there'd be a different world, one in which the Saxons had regained their kingdom, or one in which they would have lost it forever.

Edward and I quickly decided we had to speak with Father and knowing he'd be with Cerdic Guthweinson, putting the final touches to his plans for the march and coming battle, we hurried off to find him. He had a small hut that he jokingly called his Official War Room down on the training grounds and sure enough he and his commander were inside. They were studying a large box of sand that they'd used to make a rough map showing the roads, hills and valleys of the route they'd be taking to Saint Egbert's Stone.

They looked up when we burst in without being announced and Father stood and opened his arms wide. We ran to him and he hugged us. "So why am I honoured with a visit from my two best warriors?"

We stood back and before I had time to get nervous I quickly said, "We want to come with you. We want to be part of your army."

Edward nodded vigorously and Father looked across at Cerdic and grinned. "I knew this was coming," he said and turned back to look at us. "I'm proud that you want to be part of the army, but you're still too young to fight."

"We can both carry full-sized shields now," said Edward desperately. "And we can hold our position in the shield wall."

"But can you carry a full-sized shield all day?" Father asked gently. "And can you honestly say that you wouldn't be the ... least strong part of the wall?"

We looked at each other. We knew there was only the smallest chance that we'd be taken along, but we didn't want to give up yet. "I'm sure we'd try to be the best warriors on the field," I said. "And if the wall was broken, we wouldn't be the first to fall."

Father ignored this and smiled at us. "I called you my best warriors just now for a reason. You *are* my best warriors, or at least I'm convinced that you will be ... one day. But now you're still too young and the lives of my soldiers depend on the strength of the wall. If one part is breached, then the Danes will break through and all will be lost. Do you want that to happen?"

We both looked at our feet. "No, Father," we said quietly.

He hugged us again. "Then stay here in Athelney with the garrison I'll be leaving to defend it.

And be on your guard, in full armour and carrying your full-sized shields. If we lose this battle and any of us live, we'll be retreating back here and you'll need to defend the walls from the Danes who'll be chasing us."

"Yes, Father," we answered and I looked up and held his eye. "No Dane will take Athelney while we live."

He nodded. "I don't doubt it. Now come to the map box and help me and Guthweinson decide the tactics for the battle."

The night before the thousand set out I didn't think I'd be able to sleep, but I woke up to the sounds of the warriors getting ready to march. We royal children all scrambled to get dressed in the full armour we trained in every day. Edward and I proudly hefted our full-sized shields and led the way through the hall and out into the sunshine.

But when we got outside and looked down on the training grounds where the thousand were smartly drawn up in disciplined ranks, there was none of the excitement and ceremony we'd expected. A Christian priest prayed over them and sprinkled them with holy water, but unlike in the first raid against the Danes the atmosphere was tense and quiet. Looking back on the earlier actions, I suppose they were simple acts of defiance against an oppressor, but now we were marching to a full-blown war. Once the thousand had joined with the thousands of the fyrd we'd be striking back with everything we had; we'd be making a bid for total victory and in doing so we were risking the entire future of the kingdom. If we failed it was unlikely that we'd rise again.

My mother stood a little way off in her full royal persona and with that same sense of strange power that she'd had about her before the very first raid Father had led against the Danes. She was wearing what finery she had left and holding herself with the pride and dignity of a queen of Wessex and a daughter of the powerful Saxon House of Mercia. As had happened on the first raid, my father raised his axe in salute and she bowed her head regally.

Then with a snapped order, the thousand marched off. The housecarles who were being left behind as the defending garrison formed an honour guard lining the way to the main gates, and all of us watched until the last soldier had disappeared through the gate and out into the marshes.

It was then that I realised there was no sign of Ara anywhere.

The rest of the day settled into a deep sense of anticlimax. I had no doubt that soon we'd be tense and deeply worried about the outcome of the battle and afraid for the soldiers who'd be fighting in it, but for the moment Athelney seemed as empty as a barrel after all the good things had been taken out of it.

Edward, Mouse and I went to train with the garrison, but none of us seemed able to give it any real effort. We soon gave up and went back to the Little Palace and decided we were bored. We stayed bored for the rest of the day and as the curlews called their lonely cry and the darkness descended on the marshlands, we went to bed.

Father had reckoned on three days to reach Saint Egbert's Stone and then, after the fyrd had been properly gathered and forged into one with his thousand warriors, the next task would be finding and fighting the Danish Great Army.

But we'd heard nothing for almost five days now. Ara had reappeared but had nothing to say about the coming battle. She hardly functioned as our nurse now: she would make sure little Aethelfryth was all right and had what she needed and would then take herself off again.

I convinced myself that I understood how she felt. None of us waiting in Athelney could do anything other than watch the ways through the wetlands for signs of messengers bringing news. And if we spoke to anyone at all, it was only to go over the same few facts we had and then try and guess what was about to happen. But none of us knew, of course. Far better to keep out of the way and wait until whatever was destined to happen finally did happen.

Night came around quickly again, and it was almost with a sense of relief that we retreated to our sleeping places. This time Ara didn't even bother to make the effort to appear and help little Aethelfryth get ready for bed. Instead I tried to help my sister undress and put on her nightgown. She told me proudly that she didn't need any help, but then ended up with a fit of the giggles and I had to help her escape from a tangled knot of sleeves. I settled her down with her doll and watched as she swiftly dropped off to sleep.

Edward seemed to be asleep too, wrapped up in his blankets like a hedgehog layered in leaves during his winter hibernation. But I knew I'd be awake all night worrying and waiting for news. Mouse kept me company, snuggling up to keep me warm and listening to all my whispered worries.

I woke up to a deep darkness. The fire in the central hearth had sunk to the faintest glow of embers and the shadows were so dense they seemed almost textured like cloth. I don't know what had woken me, but then I heard the deep-throated chuckle of a raven and looked out to see a darker shadow moving towards me. It was Ara of course.

Soon she loomed over me like a storm cloud, her eyes glittering with the same jet-like shine as those of Raarken, who sat on her shoulder.

"Wake up, Aethelflaed Cerdinga. The day of battle will soon be dawning and we have a journey to make."

I sat up, still woolly minded with sleep. "A journey ...? Where to?"

"Be patient and you will see. Hurry, the way is far and the effort great."

"It must be important," said Edward who was sitting up and scratching his head. "She's talking like a poet, a sure sign we're about to see history being made."

"You too, Aethling of the Cerdinga. You and your sister must take part in this day's destiny: it will be part of what you both will become," said Ara, and Raarken croaked quietly as though in agreement.

"Aethling of the Cerdinga ...? Do you mean me? I thought I was just Edward."

"Dress, now!" our nurse barked. "We must away ..."

"Ere break of day?" Edward suggested.

"Before dawn," Ara agreed.

"Yes, but how are we going to get there?" I asked. "It must be miles away."

"It is many leagues," Ara said. "But there are ways and roads for those who know and are blessed by the gods."

"How far is a league, exactly?" Edward asked, determined not to be overawed by Ara and her *scinncraeft*.

"Far, and you are destined to see this day's battle, so hurry."

We stumbled about in the dark, made clumsy by our sleepiness, and hampered by Mouse who insisted on trying to help and only succeeded in getting in our way. But eventually we were ready and Ara hurried us from the great hall and down to the gates of the fortress. Despite being barely awake we remembered to put on our armour and pick up our weapons and shields.

"If we're away for the day, won't somebody report us missing?" I asked.

"That is taken care of; whoever asks will be told you've gone wildfowling in the marshes."

"I've never hunted a duck in my life," Edward protested. "Why should they believe I've suddenly started now?"

"You need only know that all on Athelney will believe it," Ara replied mysteriously.

When we got to the main entrance none of the guards seemed to see us, despite the fact that everyone was being extra vigilant. I'm not even sure that the gates were opened for us, but even so we found ourselves standing on the causeway outside

Athelney, staring out over the reed beds that hissed quietly in the night wind.

"Take my hands," Ara suddenly said.

They were cold and felt like a damp leather glove full of sticks.

"Yuck," said Edward and then snorted as he realised he'd spoken out loud. "Sorry, took me by surprise."

I grinned in the darkness. You could always rely on my brother to be inappropriate. My thoughts were then interrupted by the sound of clattering wings as Ranhald joined her mate on Ara's shoulders.

"Now empty your minds of all thinking and come with me," said Ara, her voice seeming to echo over the night air.

"And just how are we supposed to do that?" asked Edward grumpily. "I'm always thinking of something – you can't just stop thought like stamping out a fire!"

"Behold ...!" Ara suddenly intoned, ignoring his protests.

"Behold! Who says 'behold' in everyday speech?" Edward moaned. Then he stopped as our increasingly mysterious nurse led us to the edge of the causeway and we looked down on a black punt that waited in the waters. "Well that looks about as inviting as mud soup."

I saw what Edward meant. The black punt looked like a darker shadow in a night of shadows, and it had an atmosphere about it that suggested it had made stranger journeys than short trips over the waters of the marshlands. Everyone knew that Ara used *scinncraeft* of course, but none of us could even guess how powerful she was. Somehow I knew that this strange black boat would take us to the battle even though it was going to be fought miles away. I also knew it would take us there quickly and in secret.

Obviously Ara's abilities as a wielder of magic had developed as much during the time she'd been in the marshes as mine and Edward's abilities to use weapons and fight in the shield wall.

I turned and looked at the strange wise woman who'd quickly become one of our greatest weapons against the military might of the Danes. "I'm happy to trust your powers, Ara," I said quietly.

"Well good, I can't say how glad I am that you're happy," said Edward irritably as he eyed the strange boat. "But I still want to know exactly where you're taking us, Ara, and why!"

"I've already said: I'm taking you to the battle."

"But why, especially after Father refused to take us with him?"

Ara was silent for a moment, but then went on, "I have been shown by the gods that you, Edward Cerdinga, and also you, Aethelflaed, will be the defenders of the land, but more importantly even than that, you will also defend an idea."

"An *idea*?" I prompted. "What do you mean? What sort of idea?"

"Not everything was made clear to me," our nurse replied. "But, I do know that from the kingdom of Wessex a sense of *identity* will grow. A sense that will be held and embraced by many people. Not only those of Saxon stock, but eventually the Danes too and after them many others who will come to these shores. Some will be invaders, others will come peacefully to live, but whoever they are they will all become part of the one idea."

I stared at the strange shadowy punt that still waited for us to step into it and tried to understand what Ara was saying. "But when will this happen?"

"Not ever if this battle against the Danes is lost. And even if we win, it will take many years, more than we could ever imagine. But you, Aethflaed Cerdinga, and you too, Edward, are part of the seed that will be planted in the soil of Wessex and will spread its roots and branches throughout the land. You must be strong and defend the idea, so that down the long, long years it may flourish and a new people be made that are not only Saxon or Dane or whatever race may come to this land, but are people of ..." She paused again as she tried to explain. "People of ... an *identity* that is beyond mere race, or religion, beyond the unimportant differences we may have ..." Her voice trailed away as she was finally defeated in her effort to explain.

"Sounds daft to me," said Edward. "But as you seem to know what you're doing, I suppose we have no choice but to do as you say."

That seemed to decide us at long last, and we finally stepped down into the punt. There then followed the long struggle to get Mouse into the boat. Now that he was too big to pick up and carry it took both of us to try and coax him down into the dangerously rocking punt and he whined pathetically. But then he gave a yelp and suddenly landed beside us in a tangle of sprawling limbs.

Ara tried to look innocent, but I knew she'd pushed him. I said nothing: sometimes drastic measures are needed when you're in a hurry. We then watched as Ara and her ravens followed. Next she took up the long pole that the marsh people use to drive such boats through the water, and pushed away from the causeway.

As soon as the punt nosed out into open water, a dense mist settled over us. The night was silent but for the gentle stirring of the reeds in the light breeze, and with the mist came the scent of green growing things and the rich black mud of the marshlands.

I have no idea how long we were in the punt or how far we travelled. Father had said he expected to take three days to reach Saint Egbert's Stone with his thousand warriors, but Ara's black punt floated through the deep darkness of the night and somehow the miles were gathered in and then left behind us, so that as dawn lightened the sky and the mist lifted, we looked out on a river that wound through a landscape of downs and fields with no sign of any reed beds or marshlands.

Perhaps I'm remembering the circumstances differently and we were far longer in the punt than

I now think. But I've gone back over the events and times in my mind and I still think that we travelled the distance in the space of a single night.

Eventually our old nurse guided the boat towards the riverbank where we climbed out and began to walk through the dawn of the day. Mouse was obviously relieved to be on dry land again and barked excitedly, but I quickly made the war-dog sign for silence and he fell into step beside me. Neither Edward nor I questioned Ara as she led us through the fields and then eventually to a rise in the land that climbed slowly up and on to a wide plain of rolling grassland. Again time and distance acted strangely as Ara kept up a constant mumbled monologue that wove itself through and around the croaks, grunts and mumbles of her ravens.

I looked at my brother and he shrugged silently. Obviously he felt the same as me; it was almost as though we were watching the making of magic as the three creatures of the old gods embroidered a sound tapestry of *scinncraeft* that was taking us to my father and his army.

Before us the wide chalk downland spread as far as the horizon with hardly a tree or stand of gorse to break up the long rolling undulations. Far above us buzzards circled, their high fierce calls torn to sound ribbons by the wind. But then I thought I caught a different noise. It was faint and distant and sounded like waves crashing on a pebbly shore.

Ara stopped and nodded to herself. "The battle-song hasn't yet begun. But it will soon."

"Is it far now?" I asked.

She smiled. "We're there."

I felt Edward's hand grab mine, and my head spun as suddenly we stood on a small rising of ground and looked out over a shallow valley. How and when we actually got there, I've no idea, but the valley undoubtedly lay before us.

At one end the land rose more steeply and there, at last, stood the Danish Great Army! Their shields were black and they all wore the same byrnie, or long leather tunic, which was studded with protecting rings and discs. Above them flew a banner showing a white horse, the personal insignia of Guthrum himself.

At the opposite end of the valley stood my father and his army. I shouted a wordless cry of greeting and Edward added his voice to mine as did Mouse.

But of course they were too far off to hear us. I could see Father standing and staring up the valley to where the Danes held their position. With him were the thousand, trained and disciplined and all with red-painted shields and shirts of mail. And around them stood the part-time soldiers of the fyrd. These carried shields of many different colours and in a wide state of repair, ranging from good to badly worn and splintered. They also wore what armour they had. Some had helmets, some just woollen hoods; some had spears, others just wooden clubs, pitchforks, or even the sickles they would have used to harvest the wheat of the season. But they stood in disciplined ranks, their shield wall already raised and joining seamlessly with the solid barrier of the thousand.

Their numbers seemed endless, filling the lower end of the valley. But the Danish army was bigger, their black shields and dark byrnies flowing over the contours of the slopes, as black and threatening as the shadow of a storm cloud. And as we watched, they sang, their deep voices rolling and swelling in a war chant as fierce as the howling of the wind and the bellowing of fighting stags.

"Look at that!" Edward whispered, his tone strung between awe and fear. "Who can stand against them? Who can stop them?"

"Father can!" I answered loyally, but my flesh crept, and as I watched them the Danes suddenly moved as one. It was a war dance, but there was nothing soft or gentle about it. Their shields opened and then rose above them as they stomped forward and then back in perfect unison, showing their discipline, showing their power, and still they sang as they flowed and swayed in a dance that made my heart pound with fear.

"Er ... wouldn't it be better if we were ... you know ... with the Saxon army?" Edward said, obviously feeling as exposed as I was. "We could be attacked."

"No one can see us," Ara answered.

"Why not?" I asked. "We're against the skyline here."

"We're the colour of the sky and the land around. If anyone sees us at all, they'll think we're a stand of gorse or small trees."

Scinncraeft again, I thought, but said nothing.

We went on watching as the Danes sang and stomped their war dance, their voices and the rhythmic beating of their spears on shields echoing over the valley.

I turned to see what my father would do, but the entire Saxon force offered only total silence and stillness to the chanting and dancing of the Great Army.

Suddenly the Danes surged forward, a great roar rising up from their ranks, but it was only a feint and they fell back in perfect unison again as they tried to draw out the Saxons and make them break their shield wall. But still our people stood in total silence waiting for the moment to strike.

Soon the quiet stillness of our army began to impress itself on the entire atmosphere of the valley. It became almost eerie, as though the Danes were not facing a force of mortal soldiers, but something else entirely, something from a place other than this middle Earth where we live.

It seemed that the Great Army felt it too, and they made a feint again, their voices clamouring to a huge pitch as though they were attempting to drown the Saxon silence. But beneath it all the silence remained, as did the stillness, and the Danes fell back once more to their original position.

"What's Father doing?" Edward asked. "Guthrum will never abandon his stand; it's too strong. They have to risk an attack."

"They will," I answered. "Just wait."

And we didn't have to wait long. As we watched, a figure stepped forward and raised his sword, glittering in the spring sunshine, then suddenly chopped it down. As one the Saxon army stepped forward and advanced, their shields overlapping like the scales on a dragon's back. But still they remained silent, despite the roaring and howling of the Danes, as they watched their enemy advance.

Father and the Saxon army walked at a steady pace, the unbroken line of shields rising and falling over the contours of the land. A charge uphill would have exhausted them before the battle had properly begun.

The Great Army feinted forward again, trying to draw the Saxon lines out, but discipline was maintained even by the fyrd who were known for their wild charge. Then when they were within a few long paces of the Danish shields a lone voice rose up and suddenly the Saxons leapt forward like a greyhound chasing a hare, a huge roar erupted from their throats at last, and they smashed into the enemy line like a battering ram.

Ranhald and Raarken added their voices to the raging din that now exploded into the air.

Shield ground against shield, sword hacked against sword and dozens of warriors fell in the opening seconds of the battle.

A gentle wind played over the valley and brought with it the mingled scents of fresh grass, wildflowers and blood. For a moment I felt sick, but then I forced myself to breathe deeply. This was the truth and reality of battle. If I was to be a shield maiden and a true Cerdinga this would be my art and my trade. If I wanted to carve a new shape for the world then I must accept the blood and damage caused by the act of doing it.

But then my attention was distracted by movement on the field and I watched as the fyrd, to the left and the right of the thousand, suddenly extended like the unfolding wings of a giant bird and swung round to attack both Danish flanks.

"I wish I was down there!" Edward shouted above the noise. "I wish I was standing with Father against Guthrum and his army!"

I watched as he danced from foot to foot and almost chewed the rim of his shield in excitement and frustration.

"Me too," I said quietly and wondered why I was so cold compared to Edward's hot-headed excitement.

"Because you think," said Ara in my ear. "And you *calculate*."

"What do you mean?" I asked, not at all surprised that she'd heard my thoughts. "I want to fight as much as Edward."

"Oh yes, I know, your brother may have the brute killing power and instinct of a wolf, but you ... you, My Lady, have the thinking ferocity of a *fox*."

I nodded. This was the first time that Ara had called me My Lady, something that underlined for me the magnitude and importance of the time. "The fox and the wolf would make formidable allies," I said.

"Indeed you will, My Lady, and the Danes will learn that lesson in the future."

I turned to look at her sharply, but then the tone of the battle's roar changed and I quickly turned back to watch as the thousand pressed forward, driving towards the White Horse banner of Guthrum's bodyguard.

Mouse barked, his huge voice echoing over the valley, and Edward and I screamed aloud in excitement and encouragement as Father and his warriors hacked and smashed their way forward. Dozens fell in the Danish wall, but there were always more warriors to bravely step up and close the breach.

I shouted and shouted until my throat burned and then ... then my head began to spin, sound and vision swirled into a muddle of tangled image and noise and then cleared, and all of us stood in the line of battle!

There was no time to think or wonder. Years of training kicked in and immediately Edward and I locked our shields into the wall of the thousand who stood to either side of us and Mouse took up his position as trained, beneath the lower rim of my shield. Ara and her ravens seemed to rise over it all, their eyes wild and raving.

"NO! NO! How can this be? This should *not* be! You're too young to fight," she shouted and raised her arms above her head as Ranhald and Raarken called and called into the chaos.

Then Edward, Mouse and I were drawn back with the thousand as they gathered themselves and then exploded forward again in a great heave against the enemy shield wall.

My entire vision was filled with the screaming face of a Dane. I drove my sword straight-armed at his gaping mouth, and as I drew it back the face sank from view.

Edward hacked at the exposed neck of a Viking as he over-reached, trying to stab my brother with his spear. The blade bit deep and the enemy fell. Mouse still stood with me, an extra weapon that protected my left side, but then I nudged him with my leg, the signal to attack when the din of battle made spoken commands useless, and with a great roar he leapt at the line of Danes. The thick spiked collar he wore saved him from a spear thrust and clamping his jaws around the Viking's throat he tore it open.

My body seemed filled with a power and strength I'd never felt before, and I wasn't afraid. There was no time for fear as I thrust and parried, smashed and hacked at the wall of Danes before me. I was aware of Edward standing next to me and as I quickly glanced at him I saw his face set in an intense grin of fury that I knew my own face reflected. This was what it was like to feel the battle-fury I'd heard the poets sing of so many times in my father's halls. This was power! This was elation! This was the heritage of the fighting Cerdingas!

The enemy line stood solid and unbroken before us and after surging back we drove forward once more with the thousand to break it. Our hedge of spears met their shields and the noise of onset rose up again. I was one part of the whole army and as one we moved in to fight the enemy. My sword rose and fell striking all who opposed me. Edward fought with a fury, his shield locked with mine, making the men of the Great Army step back before his flashing blade. Again and again I struck at the warriors of the enemy and they fell only to be replaced by others who fought with a dogged determination that was matched only by my own. Mouse fought beside me, leaping forward and using his weight to drag another Dane out of the wall.

Ahead I could see the White Horse banner of Guthrum and I joined the push towards it, Edward marching in step with me. We killed again and again as we moved forward. But the Danes held their line, reforming the wall as each of their warriors fell. My shield was hacked and battered and my sword was notched with the effort of the fight but still I fought on. Mouse covered my left side, tearing sword arms that tried to stab me and leaping bodily at the enemy line whenever they pushed back at us. And still the power of battle-fury drove us on. How long we stood there I don't know but the sun climbed slowly above us and time seemed to hang on a suspended thread.

But now Ara's voice rose in power over the noise of the fighting. "I MADE THIS *SCINNCRAEFT*! I MADE THIS MAGIC! I DO NOT ALLOW IT A MIND OF ITS OWN! NOW TAKE US BACK TO THE PLACE OF SAFETY!" And once again my head span and all noise and vision mingled in an explosion of the senses in my head. Then when it cleared we all stood once again on the rising ground above and away from the battle.

Edward and I turned to each other and after staring at the blood-spattered patterns that covered us both, we suddenly laughed aloud and hugged each other.

"So the calculating fox can feel the fury too," said Ara darkly.

"Are you surprised? Have you never seen a vixen hunting prey for her cubs?" I asked.

"Indeed I have," the wise woman replied. "And I've thanked the gods I was no victim of hers when I did."

I smiled and turned back to watch the battle, my hand resting on Mouse's broad head.

The bloody struggle went on for an entire day. Both sides standing toe to toe, the thousand against

Guthrum's warriors, as the fyrd swirled around in a fire of raging attacks that burst against the enemy shield wall and then withdrew before bursting forward again and again throughout the long hours.

But at last, as the sun sank slowly towards the horizon, the figure of my father stepped forward from the ranks of the thousand and as he raised his sword, his elite warriors formed a fighting wedge, with their king at its apex, just as they had in their first raid against the Danes. With a great roar they stabbed in a mighty thrust at the line of shields before them. The clamour of this new onset rose up above the valley, and with a great grinding screech of metal on metal, sword on sword and spear on spear, the shield wall at last broke open and the Saxons drove deep into the wound they'd made.

A roar of despair rose up from the Danes and we watched screaming in excitement as the White Horse banner trembled and then slowly fell. The Viking lines at last began to waver and then, like a sea mist before a freshening wind, the Great Army began to break apart as the warriors we once thought were invincible threw down their shields and ran!

Ara raised her arms and her voice mingled with the victory call of her ravens as the Saxons rolled forward over their enemy.

"We've done it! We've done it! The Danes are beaten! The Danes are smashed!" I screamed and then hugged Edward and danced round and round as countless numbers died far below us. Soon anyone that could still run or fight had left the battlefield. Only the dead and those too badly wounded to move now occupied the shallow valley.

I began to shiver uncontrollably even though the evening was warm, and when I looked at Edward I saw that his face was white and he too shook like someone with marsh fever.

"Every warrior pays a price for their first blooding," said Ara quietly. And taking our hands she led us away back to the river and the waiting boat.

VIII

Guthrum and his bodyguard of housecarles got away, and a good few thousand of the Viking army escaped too. They fled back to Chippenham, where my father and his Saxons besieged them for two weeks before they finally surrendered and asked for terms.

Father was generous and the Peace of Wedmore only sent the Danes into exile and forced Guthrum to accept Christian baptism with the new name of Athelstan. Father even stood as godfather to the old pirate. But here I learnt something more about the art of rule: always make an ally of your old enemy if you possibly can. As it turned out it was impossible to make an ally of Guthrum, but it had to be tried.

After this great victory the rule of the Cerdingas was re-established in Wessex. Eventually Athelney was abandoned by our court in exile and also by the people and warriors who had shared this time. But Father had already laid his plans for a church and a monastery to be built on the island in thanks for his victory over the Danes. Ara looked darkly on the men who immediately started digging the foundations for this religious complex, but she said nothing.

We departed on a bright April morning and already our changed circumstances were made obvious by the fact that we had a glittering escort of housecarles drawn from the survivors of the thousand who had stood with Father against Guthrum. When we finally left the wetlands behind, Mother gave a small chest of gold to the marsh people who had guided us back to the Roman road that led directly to Chippenham. Father also sent word that more would be sent to the marshes just as soon as the treasury had been replenished.

The journey back through Somerset was a relaxed and happy experience, in direct contrast to the night we fled from the Danes, with warm sunshine and gentle wildflower-scented breezes instead of the freezing cold and the scent of snow on the air.

The day arrived when we finally rode into sight of Chippenham's walls. The Danes had already left to go into exile in East Anglia, or to the continent to continue their raiding and pillaging. We were told that when they marched out, still carrying their weapons as agreed by the peace treaty, the Saxons watched them go in complete silence, the whole town agreeing to show them that they weren't worthy of the effort needed to throw insults. In fact the only thing that was thrown was a single clod of earth that hit Guthrum himself in the middle of his back. But the old pirate at least had a sense of his own dignity and didn't even turn to look to see who was responsible.

The town itself was in quite good repair. It isn't true that the Danes always destroyed and despoiled the settlements they invaded. In fact the gates they'd smashed through on the night Chippenham was taken had been repaired and even the houses that had been burned down had been rebuilt or were in the process of being so. This more than anything proved to Father that the Danes planned to settle in our lands and make them their own. Somebody who intends to make a new kingdom doesn't destroy the riches of the land where that new kingdom will be made once it's conquered.

When our party reached the gates and passed through into the town, we found that the people had turned out to greet us in their hundreds and they cheered loud and long as we processed along the main streets. We rode directly behind the escort of housecarles on the neat little ponies Father had sent for us. As we also wore the fine clothes and jewels that had been sent at the same time as our ponies we probably made quite an impressive sight as we waved and smiled in acknowledgment of the cheering. I'd even replaced Mouse's blood-stained battle collar with one that was studded with jewels and pearls, and he pranced proudly along like a parade horse.

Aethelgifu had spent much of the time since the defeat of the Danes literally singing the praises of the Lord of Hosts who had given us victory, and she raised her voice now to sing a stirring hymn which for some reason made the people cheer even louder.

Raarken and Ranhald then decided to join in from their place on Ara's shoulders, their raucous voices easily drowning out our sister's pious singing.

Ara herself said not a word as she strode along between Edward's and my ponies, her hands on their bridles, but she smiled secretly to herself as Aethelgifu gave up trying to compete with the ravens. A church and monastery might be being built on the island that her *scinncraeft* had helped to defend, but at least she could silence the hymn-singing that so affronted her pagan ears.

When at last we reached the wall that surrounded the palace complex we left the crowds behind. We rode through the gates into silence and for a moment we all sat quietly and stared at the mead hall we'd last seen at Christmas. Even little Aethelfryth held up her doll so that it too could see we were home again at last – or at least we were back in one of our homes. For how long we would stay there it wasn't yet clear. We dismounted and as the housecarle escort marched off, we followed Mother through the massive doors and into the hall.

For a moment we paused on the threshold staring into the space before us. Logs blazed on the central hearth, the walls were still lined with the same hangings and weavings and even the same tables and benches stood neatly stacked at the sides of the hall.

Aethelfryth suddenly let out a whoop of delight and ran across the wide flagstone floor, chased by Aethelgifu who managed a sort of restrained shuffling run, as though she thought enjoying herself might be sinful in some way.

Edward and I watched them go but didn't join in. Somehow it felt as though that sort of wild childish excitement belonged in the past for us, even though it was only four months since we'd spent Christmas afternoon chasing each other around that very hall.

"The battle has changed many things," Ara said, reading our thoughts perfectly. "Not only for Wessex itself, but for those who stood in the wall of shields too, even if it was only for a few moments."

"Have things changed so much?" I asked.

"You've defended the land and taken lives to do it: the times of childhood are no longer yours."

I nodded and Edward quietly took my hand, something he hadn't done since the day of the battle. "The next step on a long road, sis," he said.

But time has a habit of making routines, and soon we were back at our daily round of schoolwork and training as though we'd never known any different. During the months on Athelney, our lessons in Latin and Greek had stopped, mainly because the priest who'd taught us hadn't managed to escape from Chippenham. We all thought he'd been killed, but the day after we returned he suddenly appeared from wherever he'd been hiding, ready to carry on where he'd left off. Edward was deeply disappointed but Aethelgifu was delighted and I didn't actually mind that much. I enjoyed my lessons, and like Father I believe education is the key to understanding the world and all its workings. Understand the world and you can rule it better ... or at least that small part you're given to rule. Besides, Edward was stupid if he believed our teacher wouldn't have been replaced if he had been killed.

But soon we left Chippenham and went on a Royal Process, a long tour throughout the land on our way back to Winchester, the capital of Wessex, where Father had one of his main palaces. The journey was deliberately slow, lasting over a month, so that we could show ourselves to the people and let them know they were ruled by Saxons once again.

When we finally reached Winchester the cathedral bells rang out and the streets were packed with crowds of cheering people. I've often wondered why they seemed so joyous that the old order of Saxon thegns and overlords and royalty had come back. They don't seem to have been treated particularly badly by the Danes, once the battles had ended and their rule had been accepted. Perhaps it's because people just want to be ruled by their own folk, even if their lives are little changed by foreign rulers.

We quickly settled into our new routine and in less than two months Athelney became a memory that slowly got more and more distant. The Danes remained a threat of course, and Father began a programme of making and building towns in each region of Wessex that had strong defences and a garrison of professional soldiers. These he called 'burghs': they'd be a refuge for the people and a defensive point against the Danes if they tried to invade again. He also reorganised the fyrd, so that its training became better, and he improved its equipment, ensuring that every one of the part-time soldiers had a good shield, a spear and a helmet. If the Danes attacked again, they'd find an army of professional soldiers ready to defend the land and also a well-trained fyrd that would support them.

Both Edward and I found this defensive reorganisation and these improvements fascinating and Father often let us sit in on the meetings he had with his commanders and also the thegns who would rule the new towns. In fact learning 'statecraft', as Father called it, became an increasingly important part of our education.

As the years slowly went by our lives settled into a period of learning and growing and we came to fully fill the roles expected of us as members of the Cerdinga family. Edward became tall and strong and waited as patiently as he could for the time when he'd be able to grow his man's beard. We three sisters also changed and soon I stood on the very threshold of that stage in life when the world would begin to think of me as a young woman, rather than a girl.

It was about then that we began to hear more and more about a young ealdorman called Ethelred who'd bravely fought the Danes and against all odds had protected the western part of the old Saxon kingdom of Mercia from their power.

Wessex shared a border with Mercia and Father was keen to make an alliance with this young fighter so that the two kingdoms could stand together against the Danish threat. Ethelred was invited on a state visit to Winchester and the entire town was soon in a state of uproar as preparations were made. All the damage to the gates, walls and buildings caused by the war had been repaired, and the palace precinct was smartened up with new paint and new wall hangings.

On the day that Ethelred and his party were due to arrive I got up early, spent an hour or so with Edward and Mouse training with the garrison housecarles and then I went and changed into my best and newest dress. This was made of the finest lamb's wool and was dyed a beautiful deep blue that almost seemed to shimmer in the light. Even Aethelgifu complimented me when I first tried it on, saying that it made me look almost like a Saxon queen. I also put on some of my best jewellery to give me an extra edge of confidence, dressed Mouse in his special bejewelled parade collar and finally went to the hall where Father usually received his most important guests.

Down in the town I could hear the people cheering, and rightly assumed the Ealdorman of Mercia was already being escorted through the streets and would be arriving at the palace soon. I made my way to where Father's great chair stood beneath the White Dragon banner of Wessex, ready to take up my rightful place nearby as the daughter of King Alfred. There was to be a state banquet to honour the Mercians, and sitting at the top table would give me a good view of the visitors. But as I got nearer I could see that someone was already there, sitting on the raised dais and swinging his legs. Mouse paused in mid-stride and scrutinised the figure, but before I could grab his collar in case he attacked, the dog relaxed and even wagged his tail.

"You'll need to move from there soon," I said as I walked up and guessed by his clothes that he was a high-ranking chamberlain of the Mercian court. "The king will shortly be here to receive your master."

He smiled brightly and stood up. "Yes, I know. The escort of housecarles is already in the precinct; I just thought I'd have a look around before it got too busy."

I studied him closely and decided to forgive him for not knowing who I was. He wasn't that much older than me really, and even though he had his man's beard, it was neatly trimmed and his clothes were well made and fitted him beautifully. Obviously Ethelred must value him, so it would be sensible to make friends with a man who could well be a close companion of the warrior who had kept the west of Mercia free from the Danes.

"I could show you the palace if you want," I said in an attempt to make him feel welcome.

"Thank you, I'd like that," he said smiling easily. "Beautiful hound by the way. An animal of his size must be a war-dog."

"He is," I answered simply and watched in quiet amazement as Mouse stepped forward to sniff the man's hand and then rolled over on his back like the soppiest puppy.

The man laughed and rubbed Mouse's chest in just the way my ferocious man-killing war-dog liked.

I'm not sure why I did it, but I took the young chamberlain all over the precinct, even showing him the kitchen annexe and the stables, but I have to say he was interested in everything and asked questions all the time.

"And the cooks can cope with feeding over three hundred guests at a time, you say?"

"Well yes ... as long as they don't drink too much of the strong ale before it gets served in the mead hall."

He nodded sympathetically. "Oh I know what you mean; only a month ago there was a gathering of the Mercian thegns in Tamworth. I hoped everyone would be on their best behaviour but Sigurd, the kitchen steward, had *sampled* too many of the beer barrels for quality. When he escorted the roast boar into the closing banquet, he fell over, then the servants carrying the boar fell over him, the following pages fell on to the boar, and one of them was small enough to get his head rammed up its ... well ... up its backside. And then the housecarles ran up to help, and it turned into a tug of war, with the housecarles pulling at the page's legs, and the servants pulling at the boar, and the poor page bawling like a young lamb ... well anyway, it was chaos."

I let out a snort. "Did you get into trouble?"

He grinned. "Not really: the thegns of Mercia are a rough and ready lot and they all joined in with what they obviously thought were fun and games. Even after the page had been freed they carried on for a while. It was difficult to instil a sense of dignity after that, so everyone just got drunk."

He was full of stories like that and we continued to chat as we made our way back to the mead hall.

By this time the place was packed to the rafters with soldiers and thegns and court officials. Edward and Aethelgifu were already standing behind their chairs at the top table and were watching Father and Mother parading through the hall towards their places of honour beneath the White Dragon banner. Both were dressed in their most splendid clothes and Father had on his royal regalia complete with the ancient iron crown of Wessex. But as they processed along with their best regal expressions in place, they both suddenly stopped and looked directly at me and the chamberlain.

"Ah, there you are, Ealdorman Ethelred! Where did you get to?" Father asked.

I turned with a gasp to the man beside me and watched as he bowed. "I was being conducted on a tour of your beautiful palace by your daughter, My Lord. I must say she's an accomplished diplomat and entertaining guide."

I should have been annoyed at the very least. He'd let me believe he was just a chamberlain and I'd prattled on about all sorts of rubbish. But somehow I didn't feel he was laughing at me, and when he smiled I couldn't help smiling back.

"Well I'm glad Aethelflaed kept you amused," said Father quietly and as he looked at my mother I'm almost sure I saw him wink, as though a good idea had just occurred to him. "But now we have the serious business of a state banquet to deal with," he went on briskly. "Ethelred, sit here beside me, and my daughter can sit next to you, as you find her so entertaining."

Edward caught my eye from where he stood behind his chair further down the table. Usually I sat next to him during special events like this, but this time I'd be sitting amongst the most important people in the kingdom. How times had changed. In the past Edward and I were kept apart at important events in case we misbehaved. Now we were separated because I seemed to have become part of the official welcome for the Mercian leader.

I shrugged and Edward grinned back at me. Obviously he thought I'd been clever to somehow get myself promoted to the centre of the top table and given a seat next to the main guest of the banquet, but all I'd done was to mistake an important ruler for a chamberlain. Still, I didn't mind. Ethelred was much younger and much better-looking than the kings and generals who usually came to dinner.

In the end nothing more happened between us during the banquet. Ethelred and Father spent most of their time deep in a conversation that was so quiet I couldn't hear a thing over the uproar of the mead hall. In fact I was just beginning to feel bored and wondering if I could make my way back to where I usually sat with Edward, when a silence began to make itself felt throughout the banquet. Soon it was so quiet I could hear myself breathing. Even the hounds down in the main body of the hall had fallen silent and just sat quietly waiting as though they'd been given the order to do so.

I looked up and saw Ara filling the hall with her dark presence and slowly walking towards the top table. Both Raarken and Ranhald sat on her shoulders, and she was holding Aethelfryth's hand. My sister walked with dignity beside her, completely unaware of the awe people felt for the wise woman who was her nurse. In fact, Aethelfryth was now about as old as I was when we'd fled to Athelney and didn't really need looking after in the same way, but I don't think anyone dared tell Ara this. Also my sister didn't seem to mind, so why kick a hornets' nest when you can step quietly round it?

At one point on her journey towards the top table, Ara was forced to wait because a bench had been pushed out into the aisle between the tables, blocking her path. But as soon as the people on the bench realised that Ara was standing silently behind them, they all scrambled to their feet and dragged it out of the way. The old woman walked on without a word while her ravens glared about them and croaked to each other as though discussing the guests.

I watched as she continued on her way until she stood before the king and queen. "I have brought your youngest daughter, sir and madam," she said, her voice rising into the rafters and seeming to echo over the entire hall. "She too is a Cerdinga and deserves her place at the high table."

Father nodded. "Indeed she does, Ara. I quite agree."

The old woman nodded as though finding the king's behaviour acceptable. "She deserves all due respect ... there may be a time when those of her blood who are yet to be born will rule a kingdom greater in size than your own, Alfred Cerdinga. Though your name and your deeds will be considered greater still."

I heard an intake of breath over the entire mead hall as though all the guests shared one set of lungs. But Father just nodded slowly then said, "Aethelfryth may sit next to her mother, and you may join us also, Ara-of-the-Ravens. I'm sure a place can be found for you."

"I am but a simple woman, Alfred Cerdinga: there should be no place at your high table for the likes of me," she answered and before anything more could be said, she turned and walked along the length of the table until she stood at the halfway point between Edward and me. Mouse slipped from under the table where he'd been lying at my feet and stood wagging his tail as Ranhald and Raarken cackled at him in greeting.

"Greetings, My Lady Aethelflaed and My Lord Edward," Ara said. "I have come to tell you that I had a dream in the daytime that told of your futures, but the meaning was borne away before I could commit it to memory."

"Waste of time telling us then," I heard Edward mutter.

"Not entirely," Ara said turning her black eyes on him. "I have a shadow of a thought remaining, that tells of alliances and glories, though where and when I cannot say. But know this, all of you now present in this hall, that Alfred King of Wessex may now be laying the foundations of a mighty future, but it is those who come after him that will build its walls and cap it with a roof that will withstand any storm sent against it."

Her voice rang out into a deepening silence and when I was sure she had nothing more to add I nodded at her. "Thank you, Ara," I said, suppressing a shudder that ran up my spine. "If that is the shadow, then how much greater must be the deed?"

"Don't you start speaking like a poet too," Edward hissed despairingly. "If I want an ordinary conversation, I'll have to start talking to myself soon!"

Ara ignored him and after bowing to each of us she turned and slowly walked down the length of the hall and out of the main doors.

It took a few moments for the noise to return to its usual levels of clamour, but when it did I looked along the table and called down to Edward. "It looks like we're destined to have a successful future!"

"Well of course," he answered dismissively. "We're the children of Alfred Cerdinga and Aelswith of Mercia. Anyway, Ara has said something like this before, at our first battle."

"But then she was only talking to *us*: we were the only ones to hear. This time I think she wanted to let everyone know what we had to do, and this time she was talking about something specific, not just some idea about what the country could become."

"Well it wasn't that specific ... what was it? 'Alliances and glories' ... what alliances and glories? If her prophecies are going to be of any use, they've got to be more detailed than that!"

I nodded. He was right of course, but now Ara had placed me and Edward at the very centre of some future purpose, and she'd made sure that everyone of importance had heard about it.

That night as I lay in the darkness I found myself admiring Ara's sense of style. She had the same timing and delivery as the best poets who sang in the halls of the palace. And though she didn't wear beautiful robes and sing to the accompaniment of musical instruments, she *was* clothed in the mystery of herself and had the living instruments of Ranhald and Raarken to accompany her words and *scinncraeft*.

In her own way, Ara was one of the greatest artists of the kingdom of Wessex and therefore of the entire Saxon world. I needed to remember that.

Ethelred's visit ended not long after that and though I saw him quite a few times more before he left and even sat in on some of the discussions he had with Father, I never got a chance to talk to him alone again. I was disappointed at first without really knowing why, but I soon got over it and continued with my usual routine.

Since the Battle of Eddington the Danes had kept behind the borders of Danelaw, which was the name they gave to the lands they ruled now as agreed in the Peace of Wedmore. In fact most of the Great Army had sailed over the sea to fight on the continent and while they brought war and destruction to others, we Saxons strengthened our armies, built the defensive towns called 'burghs' that gave our kingdoms a network of military strongpoints, and generally prepared for the end of the peace, which we knew must come.

Both Edward and I were now an accepted and integral part of the army, but Aethelgifu and

Aethelfryth no longer trained, choosing instead different routes through life. Aethelgifu became more and more involved with the Church while Aethelfryth, who was growing up quickly, was more interested in any babies she could find, helping to look after and play with them whether the mother wanted her involvement or not!

So our lives continued in a round of the familiar and the peaceful. But then one day in the year 885 the news we'd all been dreading and expecting came to our halls. The Danish Great Army had come back to our islands. They'd crossed the seas and had landed in East Anglia, the realm held by Guthrum. We all of us knew that the time had come to defend our lands again.

The messenger had arrived in the early morning and strode into the palace bringing with him the scent of the wild flowers of the season, and also a sense of dread that filled the streets with muttering groups of worried citizens. Somehow the people always knew whether the news was good or bad when a messenger arrived in Winchester, even if they didn't know the exact details.

Edward and I were soon called to a war council and as we met in the corridor that led to the council chamber, we immediately began to discuss what might happen.

"Father will call out the fyrd straight away," Edward said decisively. "And send them in support."

"Yes, but where to?" I asked as we hurried along, collecting a gaggle of chamberlains and officials in our wake. "Did the message say if the Great Army was marching and if so, did it say where it was heading?"

"I suppose that's what we're going to find out now," he answered.

I also expected Father to immediately call out the fyrd and get ready to march but sometimes this didn't happen. If the part-time soldiers were all called from their jobs before they were truly needed then trade would suffer and the country could be impoverished. As Father said 'defending the land and feeding the people is a fine balance'.

The council chamber was one of the biggest spaces in the entire palace, second only to the mead hall. It was so important that not only was the floor paved with granite, but there were even stone columns with round-topped arches that held up the main beams and rafters of the roof above us.

I think Father liked to think that it looked like a Saxon version of the old Senate of Ancient Rome. Though in truth none of us really knew what that'd looked like.

When myself and Edward arrived, the double rows of benches that lined the long walls of the rectangular chamber were already full of army commanders, thegns and the entire 'Witan', or council of elders, whose job it was to advise the king. The place smelled of the pitch torches that studded the walls and of wood smoke rising from the hearth that blazed in the centre of the floor.

Father's great chair stood beneath the stone arch at the top of the chamber, with two smaller chairs on either side of it for Edward and me. We both hurried forward and sat down to wait for the king amidst a low buzz of worried conversation. Whenever the Danish Great Army came to our shores there was always years of war to fight before there was any hope of regaining peace, and everyone in the chamber knew it.

When Father finally did arrive there was no ceremony. He was deep in conversation with Cerdic Guthweinson and they continued talking as they crossed the chamber and took their places, Father sitting and talking over his shoulder to Cerdic, who stood behind his chair.

We all waited in silence until at last the king nodded and turned to face the room. He sat quietly for a moment as he looked around at the people who helped to rule Wessex. Then he finally drew breath and said, "There's not much to say. You all know that the Danish Great Army has landed again and threatens Saxon borders. All thegns here will return to their lands after this gathering and call out the fyrd; you'll then march to Guildford where the army will muster. The call has been sent out to all areas as well as to Ethelred of Mercia." He paused and the grim expression on his face relaxed until I thought I could see the ghost of a smile playing around his lips. "Last time the Danes caught us unprepared, but this time it'll be different: we have more housecarles, the fyrd is better trained and equipped and most towns are armed with better defences and strong garrisons. Guthrum has taught the Saxon people many valuable lessons, but now it's time he realised his pupils have become far greater than their teacher!"

I listened to the cheers echoing through the council chamber and smiled. Sometimes a ruler could achieve more with quiet and relaxed confidence than any number of speeches of fire and fury.

IX

As members of the ruling House of Cerdinga we could have ridden to battle on horseback. But what would have been the point? An army only marches as fast as its slowest soldier, so we wouldn't have reached the Danes any earlier. And if we wanted to prove that by having horses we were in some way superior to any other Saxon, they'd only have to see us bleed in battle and, in time, die of all the things that kill every other human being, to know that we were no better than and no different from everyone else.

Father led the way, setting a pace that covered the ground at a reasonable rate, but which wouldn't exhaust his warriors before they'd even had a chance to fight. I marched with Edward and Mouse near the head of the column that wound its way through the green countryside of Wessex. The road followed the high ground, so was dry and firm and as I turned to look back over our ranks I could see the army stretching back into the distance, as long and as sinuous as a serpent. Above us flew the White Dragon banner, the symbol of Wessex, and beneath it stepped the thousand, the elite veterans of the Battle of Eddington. These were the core of the army and would be the anchor of the shield wall when we raised it against Guthrum and the Danes. Behind them came the much larger contingent of the fyrd, marching almost as smartly as the professional soldiers and now each equipped with a good shield, spear and helmet. They were no longer the rabble of former times, but trained fighters with a determination to end the Danish threat for good.

I turned back to face the front and tried to ignore the small knot of excitement in my stomach because it had nothing to do with war. But it was no good; Ethelred of Mercia would be joining us at the muster in Guildford and I could hardly think of anything else. Well ... that wasn't strictly true ... Guthrum's ugly face would keep floating up and getting in the way of the Mercian lord's bright smile, twinkling blue eyes and neatly trimmed beard, but with an effort I could usually push aside the old pirate's image and concentrate on the much more pleasing picture of our ally!

"Why do you keep sighing?" Edward suddenly asked, taking me by surprise.

"What ...? Oh, I'm just thinking about ... about home ... and ... and the need to keep the Danes out!"

"Fair enough. I suppose we're all thinking about that, but you look like you've got a stomach ache or something."

"Only the guts of the Danes should feel pain on this day ... the pain of a Saxon sword deep in their innards."

Both of us jumped away from the dark shape that had suddenly appeared between us.

"Ara! Can't you wear a set of bells or something, so we can hear you coming?" my brother shouted.

The ravens, Ranhald and Raarken, in their usual place on the old woman's shoulders, both gave cackling croaks that sounded suspiciously like laughter, and even Ara's frown-creased face lightened for a moment. "Perhaps I should sing one of Aethelgifu's hymns."

"I wouldn't go that far," said Edward grumpily. "A gentle cough would do."

Ara said nothing, the silence stuffed with the sort of atmosphere that only the wise woman could pack into it.

"Anyway, what are you doing here, Ara?" Edward finally asked. "Does Father know you're marching with us?"

"Where else would he expect me to be? I stood with him at Eddington, and I will stand with him in every battle from now until I'm finally called to the halls of the gods."

"And ... er ... is that going to happen any time soon?" Edward asked innocently.

"When Wotan decrees."

"No hints or details at all, I suppose."

"The gods will act in their own good time."

"I see," said Edward. "Well if you get any, you know, *inklings*, just give us the nod and perhaps we can arrange a little send-off of some sort. You know the sort of thing, a few ales, a few funny stories and memories ..."

Ara stared at him in silence.

"Then again, perhaps not." Edward stumbled on. "Not right to celebrate a death ... I suppose ..."

The voices of Ranhald and Raarken were raised in what sounded like dark disapproval as we marched on towards Guildford.

The weather was kind to us and we made good time. Watching the fields, woodlands and pastures of Wessex unfold about us as we marched I understood why the Danes wanted to carve out new lands for themselves on these islands. The earth was rich, the weather usually kind and gentle, the harvests good. What more could a man or woman ask of their home? The only disadvantage to living in such wealth and comfort was the need to defend it from those who would take it from you.

Guildford had been raised to the status of one of Father's new burghs and its improved defensive dykes and ditches were still raw and without grass cover as we approached. There were also high palisades along the top of each mound that surrounded the town and housecarles were clearly visible as they patrolled the fighting platforms that ran along behind the wooden walls.

The people of Guildford greeted us with wild excitement as we marched through the gates. Usually a town has mixed feelings about a fighting force of our size suddenly descending on them and filling the place with soldiers who would all need feeding, but with Guthrum and the Danish Great Army on the rampage nearby, we were all very welcome.

Ethelred and his force hadn't yet arrived, but they were expected in the next day or so. The town was obviously well prepared for its role as the muster point for the royal army. It was well provisioned with supplies and had also designated large areas of open land beyond the walls as places for military camps.

Of course Father and his commanders, as well as Edward and me, were invited to a feast. But once again nobody got too excited during the eating and drinking in the town's official mead hall. After all, Guthrum and his army were still to be fought, and who could even guess how that would go?

Father politely accepted the town's offer to make the head ealdorman's home his headquarters, but Edward and I were glad to get back to the camp that had been pitched beyond the town walls.

To be honest our well-appointed tents that we'd inspected before the campaign began were far more comfortable than the hovels that were the best some towns could offer.

The next day dawned bright and clear and I was soon up and dressed in my full military gear. Any veteran housecarle would probably say that it's better to conduct everyday business when on campaign in a more comfortable outfit of everyday wear, rather than stomping around carrying a heavy shield and weapons. But something made me put on the full regalia I'd had made for the coming battles. The mail shirt fitted me perfectly, accentuating the fact that I was now a young woman in a way that I didn't mind at all. The helmet too was a beautiful piece of work with delicate gilding around the rim and nose guard, and the fact that it was a strong piece of equipment that could turn a blow from a Danish axe only added to its beauty for me.

I then strapped on sword and dagger, picked up my shield, decorated with the White Dragon of the Royal House of Wessex, called Mouse to heel and set out into the early-morning light. Everywhere I walked the soldiers of both the elite one thousand and also the fyrd saluted me as I passed, something I found deeply pleasing. I returned the salutes with a suitably stern face and strode purposefully through the smells of wood smoke, frying griddle cakes and bacon towards the perimeter of the camp. I had no idea what I'd find there, but I hoped I looked impressive.

When I reached the picket lines I made a great show of inspecting the sentries on duty, but eventually I would have to admit to myself that I was checking the defences on the side nearest to the road that led directly from Mercia because I hoped to be the first to see Ethelred and his army arrive.

It was precisely at that moment that I looked along the road for the umpteenth time and there was the banner of Mercia, the Yellow Wyvern, emerging through the wispy mist.

If Aethelgifu had been there I'd have asked her to say a prayer of thanks for me. As it was I sketched a quick thank you to whoever was the saint of the day, and immediately strode forward to meet Ealdorman Ethelred, Lord of the Mercians.

I slung my shield on my arm and even drew my sword and stopped in the very centre of the road with Mouse standing impressively by my side as I waited for the advancing army to notice me. In fact I must have made quite a sight, because as the army paced out of the mist, they immediately came to a halt and stood in silence.

Slowly I raised the hilt of my sword to my forehead in salute, and then swung it down and held it at what I hoped was rather a fetching angle, away from my mail-clad figure.

I then watched as Ethelred stepped forward from the ranks. He too was in full battle array and looked just as I imagine the young god Thunor would have looked before striding into combat.

"I see you carry the noble device of Wessex on your shield, but who do I have the honour of addressing?" he called.

"One you know," I replied.

"A shield maiden, I see, and high-ranking, but which one of that kind marches in the army of King Alfred?"

I sheathed my sword and then removed my helmet.

A short silence followed that was suddenly broken as Ethelred laughed. "The king's daughter, I see. Greetings, Princess Aethelflaed."

"Greetings, Ealdorman Ethelred," I answered, then said with formal politeness, "You are very welcome as part of the army that will defeat Guthrum and his pirates."

Ethelred sketched a polite little bow and smiled, his face alight. "Thank you, My Lady. I'm glad to be part of any army that counts you among its ranks."

I hurriedly put my helmet back on to hide my blushes. Sometimes it's easier to deal with insults than compliments. Then I marched with Ethelred at the head of his army as they entered the town and were cheered by the population who were still afraid enough of Guthrum to be relieved when they saw more Saxon soldiers arriving.

When we arrived at the ancient 'moot tree' where legal disputes had been settled for literally centuries – or so the people of Guildford claimed – I still walked with him, matching him step for step. He approached my father who, as the 'bretwalda' or war leader for the coming battle, waited to greet him formally.

It was hard to tell what Father thought about me taking it upon myself to meet and then march with Ethelred, but he smiled happily at us both and seemed very pleased about something.

Of course there was another feast of greeting that night in the town's mead hall, putting more pressure on Guildford's supplies. However, Ethelred had had the good grace and foresight to bring supplies along with him, which helped with costs and made him very popular with the locals.

"How do you like Mercian meat, My Lady?" he asked during the meal.

What sort of answer could I give to that? "It's ... er ... it's very nice ... juicy!" I managed at last and tried to ignore my toes, which were curling with embarrassment.

Father had made a great show of sitting me next to Ethelred when the feast began, but the effort was completely wasted because I couldn't think of anything interesting to say, and anyway the ealdorman spent most of his time discussing battle tactics with Father. Just like last time.

Edward was sitting further down the table, but he still managed to catch my eye and grin while doing something obscene with a carrot on his plate. I soon felt a little better when I threw an apple down the table and it hit him with a really satisfying clunk.

Edward rubbed his head frowning, but he was soon grinning again and mouthed 'Good shot!' at me. Males may be irritating, but sometimes brothers aren't *too* bad.

X

For the next few days the army waited for the scouting parties to come back with news of Guthrum. The combined forces of Wessex and Mercia numbered over ten thousand fighters, so we'd have to move soon if Guildford was going to have any food supplies left to see them through the next winter.

Training went on to keep everyone battle-ready, but then Father decided that I should practice with Ethelred and his war band. He never explained why, just smiled secretly to himself and nodded encouragingly. I must admit I've never felt such an excruciating mix of emotions! I was both excited and terrified at the same time. What if I made a fool of myself? What if Ethelred decided I wasn't good enough to fight with his elite warriors? He was too experienced a soldier to let me take a position in his shield wall if I wasn't up to standard; he wouldn't risk the lives of his fighters.

But I needn't have worried. His war band soon accepted me and I held my position in the shield wall without any difficulty, as did Mouse, protecting my left side and leaping out to seize whichever poor soul was playing the enemy whenever the opportunity arose. I'd originally been given a place in the battle formation next to Ethelred himself, probably because it was felt he might need to protect me, the daughter of his paramount ally, but when he saw I was a capable fighter it was generally agreed that I'd earned my place of honour as a warrior.

What can I say? Even though Guthrum and the Great Army were once again threatening our lives and our lands, I was happier than I can ever remember being! I trained every day with Ethelred and his soldiers, who all treated me with respect and as a warrior with an equal standing to their own. And life was exciting, with a purpose beyond the usual round of the everyday and the ordinary. I even think

I'd have been content if the situation had continued like that indefinitely.

But then one day the scouts who'd been sent out to find the enemy returned, and their reports were urgent. Guthrum and the Great Army were besieging Rochester, and though the town was resisting well behind its new defences and with its trained garrison of professional housecarles, they wouldn't be able to hold out forever.

Father, as the senior king in the alliance, called for 'Roman speed', which he duly got. The combined armies broke camp and were marching for Rochester within two hours. We left Guildford at dawn without any ceremony and as it was so early there were very few citizens up and about to see us go.

The weather had been fine and dry for more than a week and the roads were good and mud free, which is why we reached Rochester within four days, a breathtaking speed. On Father's orders I'd marched with the Mercians and though I stayed close to Ethelred, there was little time for idle chat. He was constantly busy, walking up and down the line, giving orders and asking for reports. I watched keenly as he directed his field army; I wanted to know everything there was to know about commanding a fighting force and here I had a master of the craft to learn from.

Rochester is one of the principle towns on the River Medway and the Great Army had sailed their fleet of dreaded dragon boats right up to its defences and beached them below its walls. We caught the enemy by surprise and as we were already in battle formation we hardly paused as we marched over the hills surrounding the Medway valley and charged down on their siege lines.

Any lesser force would have broken and fled if they'd found themselves unexpectedly confronted by an army of over ten thousand warriors. But this was the Danish Great Army; every one of its fighters was battle-experienced and as tough as boiled leather. When our war horns growled out their challenge, the enemy commanders barked orders and their entire force wheeled about as smoothly as cogs in a machine and faced us with shields locked and spears levelled.

Then the singing began: their voices were fierce and deep and rolled around the valley like the roaring of a mighty beast that had somehow developed a sense of rhythm. Our reply was simple and sharp, a single word spat out again and again like a hail of arrows.

"*OUT!* Out! Out!"

"*OUT!* Out! Out!"

"*OUT!* Out! Out!"

We hit them at a dead run, our shields locked, our spears a deadly hedge of razor steel. The thundering crash as we met echoed around the hills and we drove forward like a battering ram deep into their lines. My spear shattered in my hand and I drew my sword to hack again and again at the wall of shields before me. The Great Army gave back before our ferocity, but then a huge shout went up from their lines and with a heave they pushed against us, dug their feet into the ground and stood like a mighty rock before our storm.

Shield wall crashed against shield wall and neither side gave back. As each warrior fell, another stepped over their body to take their place in the wall. My sword arm ran red, beside me Ethelred fought with the power and cunning of a wolf, and Mouse ran in to bring down man after man.

But the force of our charge had been absorbed and our momentum was lost. Now it was a battle of endurance. Which side would break first? It seemed we fought for hours and still neither would give ground. My world was reduced to the few metres I could see clearly around me. I killed again and again and still the enemy stood and answered violence and rage with rage and violence. It seemed that nothing would ever change and we'd fight on until we too fell to the axe, spear or sword.

But then even over the din and rage of the battle I heard harsh, deep voices calling, and there above me I saw two ravens flying black against the pristine blue of the sky.

"Ranhald and Raarken!" I shouted, and they circled over me, calling and calling. A living Raven banner.

"Let us break this line of skraelings and outlanders," a voice said in my ear and I turned to see Ara beside me, her grey hair wild in a wind that nobody felt, her black eyes bright with a fire of power.

She leaned towards the enemy and spat a word I couldn't catch and two Danes immediately fell. Perhaps unseen arrows had hit them, perhaps they slipped on blood-slick grass; I have no other explanation.

"Ara, what are you doing here?" I shouted over the din.

"Fighting, My Lady," she answered and smiled in a way that made her face look like a skull.

Ranhald and Raarken now dropped from the sky to land on her shoulders, and as she strode forward, the enemy began to recede before her, a look of terror on their faces as the pagan Danes recognised a wise woman of power. Ethelred, being the good commander he was, seized the moment and advanced beside Ara and our shield wall followed.

Now the wise woman raised her arms above her head and let out a shriek that stabbed through the air like a blade. Almost immediately there was an answering roar and somehow I knew that the soldiers of Rochester had opened their gates and were attacking the Great Army at the rear.

To my left I could also see the White Dragon banner of Wessex driving forward, and as our two ravens flew up into the air, their voices raucous and challenging, the Great Army let out a despairing roar and ran.

Now began a deadly chase, and many of the enemy scrambled down towards the river and their dragon boats that lay drawn up on the banks.

"DON'T LET THEM ESCAPE!" A huge voice bellowed. "BURN THEIR SHIPS! BURN THEIR SHIPS!" It was then that I realised the voice was mine, and that the soldiers around me were obeying what they'd taken to be an order.

I led the way with Ethelred and Mouse beside me, and as the broken enemy fell and scrambled down on to the riverbank they turned to fight. We didn't even pause to redress our ranks, we just smashed into them, driving them back into the water and slaughtering them in their hundreds.

Now Ara appeared again, a blazing torch held high in each hand and Ranhald and Raarken flying above her. With a wordless cry she threw one of the torches into the nearest ship and it immediately burst into flames. Her hands were somehow never empty of flaming torches and she handed them out to the warriors that clamoured about her, and who then ran to throw them into the beached ships. Soon over half of the Great Army's fleet was ablaze.

But the Danes are fierce and tough fighters, and despite our best efforts, many escaped in the dragon boats that remained. Those warriors left on land, after the initial rout, reformed their lines and began a fighting retreat that lasted for the rest of the day.

Then as the sun began to set over the land, Father finally called off his army and we stood and watched as the enemy slipped away into the gathering shadows. I found that I was still standing with Ethelred and his Mercians and not knowing that I spoke aloud I said, "What will happen now? Where will they go?"

"I think Guthrum still lives," Ethelred answered. "He'll lead his army back into East Anglia where they'll reform and attack again."

"Even after we've beaten them?" I asked, feeling suddenly exhausted.

"Oh yes, the Great Army isn't like other fighting forces: you can't destroy it completely. It's like a dragon of legend; if you cut off its head it'll crawl away and grow another and then breathe fire at you again."

"So what can we do?" I asked as the elation of our victory began to drain away.

"Fight them again," Ethelred answered quietly. "And then again and again, until it finally gets tired of growing new heads and goes away to find other victims."

"But that can't be right," I said feeling anger rising to a new pitch of outrage within me. "We must find a new way of killing it ... or ... or perhaps of taming it and making it harmless."

"Harmless?"

"Yes," I said and then paused as I slowly thought my way forward through the exhaustion of battle. "In parts the Danes have settled on this island ... made it their own, whether we like it or not. They've mixed their blood with our people's, and these new children, born of this mixing, are part of us. But they have to be *made* part of us. Their new lands and settlements must become part of our lands and settlements ... and ... and I suppose we must become part of theirs too."

"And how would you make this happen? How *could* you make this happen?"

"In a way they would understand and couldn't deny. By battle and conquest. But after that ... I don't know ... by alliance ...? By friendship ...?"

Ethelred turned to look at me squarely, his armour was battered and bent, he was covered in blood and he looked as exhausted as I felt, but suddenly he laughed and seized me in an embrace. Then he stood back and raising his voice so that the entire Mercian army could hear, he shouted:

"Behold Aethelflaed, princess and daughter of Wessex! Shield maiden and tamer of dragons!"

At first I thought he was making fun of me, but then he dropped to one knee and bowed his head like a man before his queen. And before I could do or say anything in reply a strange murmuring rumble began to grow and swell on the air, getting gradually louder and louder until it seemed that the entire day was filled with a massive rhythmic thundering as each and every Mercian soldier beat their swords, axes and spears on their shields in salute.

XI

My fancy ideas about making the Danes and Saxons already living on our island one people would have to wait. First we had to defeat the Great Army once and for all. And so began a campaign that would last on and off for years, but which filled our lives to the brim in the following months.

Immediately after we'd broken the siege of Rochester, the combined armies of Wessex and Mercia fell back on Guildford and after sending out scouts, we waited to see what the Great Army would do next. We didn't have to wait long and soon we were shadowing the Danes in a long chase that saw many skirmishes but no decisive battle.

Guildford became our main base of operations, but this time Father had learnt a valuable lesson from Ethelred when he and his army had first arrived with their own food. He ensured the town was well supplied by settlements throughout Wessex.

It was a strange time, one of long periods of fighting and marching, followed by briefer times of rest, usually within the protecting walls of Guildford. One night Mouse, Edward and I were sitting in the great hall of the house we used when we were there, and in an attempt to follow our usual rule of not talking about the war if we could help it, we sat chatting idly about the family.

"It's finally happened then," said Edward. "Aethelgifu's gone into a convent at last. At least we won't have to listen to her droning on about God any more."

We'd just finished supper and I was feeling comfortable and drowsy as I tried to stretch my legs out towards the central fire without looking like some old battle-hardened housecarle. "Don't be mean," I said, determined to defend our younger sister. "She didn't only talk about God."

"No, I suppose not," Edward admitted. "Sometimes she'd stretch herself to talking about praying and the next church service."

"She'd also tell you that you wouldn't get into heaven and that the devil had a place especially prepared for you in the fiery pits."

"True," Edward agreed. "Though I seem to remember that you weren't going to do much better. What was it ...? 'Aethelflaed, you'll be a handmaiden to the lesser demons and spend eternity cleaning up their dung'."

"Something like that, yes. She had a charming turn of phrase when she put her mind to it," I replied and poked Mouse with my toe. He was lying on his back with his paws in the air and playfully tried to chew my shoe as I continued to prod him.

"You wait until she's an abbess of her own convent," Edward went on. "She'll run the place like an army camp and all the nuns will have to pray on their knees in ranks, like a grovelling shield wall to God."

"Who's this you're talking about?" a voice suddenly asked and we turned to see Ethelred striding across the hall towards us.

"Aethelgifu," Edward said as he pushed out a chair for the Mercian leader with his foot. "She's gone to be a berserker for God."

"A what!?"

"She's become a nun, or at least a novice," I explained. "She'll take the full vows later."

"Oh, I see," said Ethelred and grinned. "I like the idea of holy berserkers though. We'd soon smash the Danes then."

"Yeah! We could send in Aethelgifu and her unit of God-nutters to soften them up first, and then we could wade in with the usual axes and swords and finish them off!" said Edward, getting animated and leaping off his chair to demonstrate, his eyes rolling and saliva drooling down his chin.

Ethelred laughed and joined in, and I had to remind myself that he was the ruler of Mercia, not just some lad a bit older than me with the same sense of humour as my brother. Then I remembered that he *was* just a bit older than me ... well ten years or so, but males are always more immature than women, and Ethelred had been forced to take on responsibility for his land when the Danes invaded. So perhaps part of him just hadn't had the chance to grow up.

This seemed to be confirmed for me when Edward and the mighty Ealdorman of Mercia fell into a weird sort of berserker dance, keeping step and leaping around me as they charged an imaginary Great Army. Mouse joined in with happy barking and capered about like a gigantic puppy as he chased along after the berserkers.

"When you've all finished ...!" I shouted over their snorts and bellowing and they collapsed into their chairs giggling uncontrollably while Mouse settled with a happy sigh at my feet. I waited for them to shut up and then asked, "Weren't you supposed to have a meeting with Father and Cerdic tonight?"

Ethelred looked guilty for a moment. "Well yes. But it was only about supplies and stuff and we've been over it so many times, so I sneaked away."

"Supplies and stuff feed the fighters and keep them strong," a voice suddenly said from the shadows and we all leapt to our feet as Ara stepped into the firelight.

She did this so often that we really ought to have been used to it, but somehow we never were and she reduced us all to quivering wrecks every time.

"Or perhaps the soldiers of Mercia live on air and water," Ara continued.

"Supplies are all arranged and the newest member of the fyrd eats as well as I do on campaign," Ethelred said calmly.

"I'm glad to hear it," the wise woman said and her ravens added their own voices in agreement.

"Have you come to tell us something important, Ara, or do you just want to torment us for your own amusement?" I asked coldly.

"Both," she answered, baring her strong teeth in a way that was as close as she came to smiling.

"Well tell us then!"

"There's not much more to add to what you already know," she said, squatting down between our chairs like an old peasant woman sorting winter turnips. "You'll have half a month to rest and then a decisive battle that will settle things ... for a while at least."

"Where?" asked Ethelred.

"When?" asked Edward.

"Who'll win?" I asked.

"As for when, I've already said," Ara snapped as she frowned at my brother. "But the battle's outcome is shrouded as always in mist and mystery, and as for *where*, I've only been shown the shadow of a once-great city, built by the Romans and straddling a river at the widest point they could bridge its waters."

"Well that could be any number of ruinous dumps," Edward moaned.

"No," said Ethelred. "The Danes want a strong base on a river that's deep and wide enough to take their dragon boats and also their trading ships. And they want it within marching distance of East Anglia. That's the Danish strategy for this part of the war. They already have the Humber and the Ouse and the Witham of Lincoln, and now after we stopped them taking Rochester on the Medway, where else is there, but the Thames?"

"And London," I added.

Discussions went on for a while longer, but soon after Ara withdrew to 'whatever slimy pit she sleeps in' as Edward put it, and Ethelred and I then took our thoughts about the Thames and London to Father. But he wasn't convinced we were right, and rather than commit the army to a march that may take it in the wrong direction he sent out extra scouts instead and waited for reports.

We were disappointed, but there was nothing we could do: Father was senior king in the alliance between Wessex and Mercia, which meant he had full command and his word was law. Still, this meant we had our two-week break as Ara had promised. I spent a good bit of it training with the Mercians, as I was still expected to march and fight with them. But even the most battle-hardened and bloodthirsty warrior can't train all day and some of the time I spent looking through the amazing library of books in the local abbey. I missed studying in the silence and peace of the great churches and I really enjoyed looking through the huge collection of writings the monks had made and copied over the years. They had almost forty books, more than even Father had, and he was known as a great scholar!

But when I felt a need for sunlight and fresh air beyond the shadows and incense of the abbey, I went back to the house we lived in and sat in the 'garden'. Well that's what the ealdorman who owned the place called it, but I knew it was nothing like the amazing and splendid gardens of ancient Rome and of the far Orient that some of the books in the abbey library told of. But even so, it was pleasant enough with many pretty flowers and plants that had been transplanted from the woodlands and hedgerows of the countryside. There was even a tiny orchard of mixed pear and apple trees, and it was here that I sat one warm afternoon with a book I'd borrowed from the abbey. I'd almost had to promise a payment in blood to be allowed to take it from the library, but after I'd reminded the monk in charge of my royal status, he eventually agreed to let me take it until the bell for Vespers was rung. This was the last service of the abbey's day and so I had a good few hours to read.

I sat under one of the trees with Mouse in his usual place at my feet and opened the book. It was a piece of military writing called *Anabasis* by Xenophon, the Greek scholar and general. It was written in the author's original language and after so many months of fighting and physical effort it was good to use my brain again. As a child I'd learnt to read and write Greek along with Latin and my own Saxon language, thanks to Father's order that great works should be translated into the 'tongue of the land'. But all of that seemed so long ago, in a distant time before Guthrum and his Great Army disrupted all of our lives.

By reading now, I felt that I was defying the Danes and their threat to our civilised world just as much as I did when I stood in the shield wall and physically fought to defeat them.

I reached the part in the book where Xenophon had proved his brilliance as a general by leading his soldiers unharmed through hostile territory, and couldn't help repeating aloud the cry of his warriors when they realised they'd reached the sea and safety:

"Thalassa! Thalassa!"

"The sea! The sea!" a voice echoed, translating the words into Saxon.

Mouse stood wagging his tail and I looked up from the page and saw Ethelred, dappled by sunlight and shadow, standing under a young apple tree. For some reason my breath caught in my throat and I coughed. But determined to seem relaxed I smiled in welcome.

"You understand Greek?" I asked, surprised.

"Of course: Mercia is a great centre of scholarship and as a son of the ruling family I was taught by the very best tutors."

"Of course," I echoed.

"And I never expected the daughter of Alfred of Wessex to be anything but a scholar herself."

"Who's your favourite writer?" I asked, genuinely interested to know what made and moved this young fighting leader of the Mercians.

"Well I prefer something with a bit of action, so Virgil's *Aeneid* is the one I like best. I'm not really interested in the philosophers like Plato and Aristotle. They just seem to like tying everything in knots and proving that black is actually white just to show how clever they are with words."

I knew he was trying to impress me with his knowledge of books and the Greek and Roman writers, but I also thought he was being honest about what he liked best. A man of action like Ethelred was far more likely to enjoy reading about a hero like Aeneas, whose descendants would include the great general Julius Caesar, than sifting through the complex arguments of philosophy. Besides, if he was trying to impress me, he was succeeding. In fact he'd impressed me almost from the first time I'd met him.

"And what about you?" he went on. "Who's your favourite?"

I held up the book I still had in my hand. "Xenophon. I feel the same as you: I'd sooner read tales about heroic deeds than the musings of any philosopher."

"Spoken like a warrior's daughter," said Ethelred with a smile.

"Not like a warrior in my own right?"

This time he laughed. He often laughed when we talked. "Oh yes! Spoken like one of the truest warriors I know!"

I put the book down, taking care that it was on the blanket I was sitting on and safe from the damp ground. "There's room here beside me," I said patting the blanket.

He sat next to me and after fending off Mouse's slobbery licks of greeting he leant back against the apple tree I'd chosen for its shade, and he breathed in the scents of the flowers and growing things. "You can understand why the Christians depict heaven as a garden."

I looked at him in surprise. "The Christians! You speak as if you aren't baptised yourself!"

"Well of course I am!" he answered defensively. "I just meant ... I just meant ..."

"You just meant that we Saxons have been followers of Christ for a few generations now, but we worshipped different gods for far longer, our own gods, not one shipped in like a batch of wine from warmer places."

"I wouldn't let the bishops hear you speaking like that," said Ethelred.

I shrugged. "I was brought up by Ara. Talk of the old religion is nothing new to me."

"Ah yes, Ara," said Ethelred. "If we had a few more like her in our ranks, we'd have defeated the Danes long ago. Perhaps the pagan Saxons were tougher than we are."

"Perhaps," I agreed. "But we're not doing so badly now. The pagan Danes ran from us fast enough at Rochester."

"That's true," said Ethelred. "But don't let's bring the war into this garden. Here and from now on, we'll only talk of peaceful things."

This was worrying; the only thing we had in common, so far, was the war and fighting. Even the books we liked were about ancient wars. What else *could* we talk about?

"Right," I said determinedly. "Peaceful things ..."

"*Mercia, his palace.*" The words came from nowhere. They just seemed to drop into my head. I'm almost sure they weren't said aloud because Ethelred was still looking at me, expectantly.

"Erm ... erm ... What's your palace like? In Tamworth ... isn't it?" I almost succeeded in keeping the squeak of desperation out of my voice.

"Yes, that's right," he answered. "It's said that Offa himself had it built. One wing is even constructed of stone."

"Offa?" I said seizing on the name of the almost mythical ruler of Mercia from the distant past. "I'd love to see the dyke he built ... clever ... the way it runs along the entire border with Wales ... In fact ... in fact it was built to keep the Welsh out, wasn't it?" I could have wept with embarrassment. Of course it had been built to keep the Welsh out! The only reason anyone would build a defensive dyke along a country's border would be to keep the people of that country out.

"*Keep going. Ask him about his hawks.*" The words dropped into my head again, seemingly from nowhere.

"Hawks!" I blurted.

"Yes? What about them?" Ethelred said, looking politely puzzled.

"You ... you train them."

He smiled brightly. "Yes, when I can. But since becoming Ealdorman of Mercia I've not really had time. You have to dedicate yourself entirely to the training of a hawk. I once had a beautiful peregrine though; she was fierce and brave and strong and, well, she reminds me a bit of you."

That was it! If I could have sunk through the ground and disappeared from view I'd have happily done so! My face was on fire and even though I wanted to run away from the entire ridiculous situation, I couldn't, because my toes were too tightly curled with embarrassment in the depths of my shoes. They were the sort of dainty court shoes I wore when I wasn't fighting the Danes. Somehow things would've been different if they'd been the tough, thick leather boots I usually wore on campaign. Then I'd be with the Ethelred I knew and understood, the Ethelred who was a war leader, a warrior, a comrade and a friend. Not this different Ethelred who was polite and socially *nice* and said pretty things in pretty ways that I just couldn't relate to.

"Tell him about the hawks your father's trained. Keep the conversation going." The words just dropped into my head again. It was almost as though someone was giving me advice. Someone who wanted me to make a success of this encounter with the new and different Ethelred. Then I understood. Then I understood completely and was annoyed enough to take back a little control.

"Well thank you for comparing me to a bird with just about enough brain to kill things, but I hope there's more to me than that!"

"That's not what I meant ..." Ethelred spluttered.

"No. I know that. But there's someone I need to see right now, so perhaps we'll meet later at training."

He left. In effect I dismissed him, proving I was still in control of at least part of my life. "You can come out now, Ara," I then said quietly.

I watched as the wise woman stepped out of the cloaking shadow she'd woven. She briefly patted Mouse's head as he bumbled up to greet her. "I was trying to help," she said quietly.

"Thank you, but I can think for myself."

"Perhaps, but when it comes to Ethelred you don't think very well."

"It doesn't matter if I think very well or not. When I have thoughts in my head, I want them to be *my* thoughts, not yours."

"Then make them the right thoughts; make them the thoughts of a woman with power and the right to rule; make them the thoughts of a queen."

She was right of course and though it had taken me a while to understand exactly *why* Father had insisted I fight alongside Ethelred and his Mercians, that didn't mean I had to behave as if I was *only* a means of making an important alliance permanent. I could still be happy with my role. I could still actually like the man I was destined to marry.

"I know what's expected of me, Ara. But it will happen when I want it to and on my terms. Stay out of my head, and stay out of Ethelred's too. Neither of us is comfortable with *your* idea of how relationships should develop. We both know what we want. At the moment we're comrades and friends and when the time is right we will take it further, but not until we're ready. Now go."

The old wise woman stood in silence for a moment, but then she finally bowed her head and walked away.

When I could no longer hear Ranhald and Raarken mumbling to each other grumpily, I breathed a sigh of relief, picked up my blanket and went to get ready for training with Ethelred.

XII

The next day the scouts came in with reports of the Great Army's movements. They were heading for London and would reach it before we had a chance to catch them. We'd been right all along. If Father had listened to us we wouldn't now have the task of breaking into a city that would be defended by some of the best soldiers the land had seen since the time of the Romans. Of course, in all reality we could equally have been wrong and we could have committed our force to protecting London while the Danes attacked Tamworth in Mercia or even Chippenham in Wessex again.

I was beginning to learn that this was the nature of war. Knowing your enemy's plans was quite literally half the battle.

Father demanded 'Roman speed' again, and the army was on the road and heading for London almost as soon as our warriors could pick up their spears. The supply wagons were already packed and waiting and everyone knew precisely what was expected of them and what they had to do. Fighting the Great Army had made us an efficient and seasoned military power. Something that I don't think Guthrum and his generals had expected.

We moved through the land like a gale and arrived in the valley of the great River Thames before the Danes had been able to fully consolidate their hold on the city of London. This was the first time that I'd seen the settlement that had been built by the Romans and in effect it was now two cities, with the new Saxon defences lying next to the crumbling walls and falling masonry of the ancient metropolis. There was a smell of burning in the air and some evidence that the population had resisted the Danes, but the broken gates and breaches in the wooden walls that lined the top of the steep defences showed that the fight to defend the city had been lost.

In fact, we'd passed lines of wagons and carts on the road, as refugees fled from London with as many of their goods and belongings as they could carry. So at least we knew there'd be few civilians to worry about when we attacked the walls.

"The Danes have not had the time to secure their new den," said Ara, arriving as unexpectedly as she always did to stand with me, Mouse and Ethelred as we surveyed the city before us.

"Shouldn't you be with the army of Wessex?" I asked as sweetly as I could. "By rights you're Father's servant, not mine."

"I serve the gods first and people second," Ara answered, not taking her eyes from the walls we'd soon be attacking. "Besides, you'll be in conference with the king soon enough. He can see my pretty face then if he misses it so much." Ranhald and Raarken cackled, obviously finding her words funny.

"Then you'd better come with us now," said Ethelred. "It'll be quick enough: we've already agreed on a two-pronged attack. We just need to decide who strikes where."

The plan certainly was quickly agreed. We Mercians were to make an assault on the northern defences with the River Thames at our back, while Father, along with Edward, would lead the army of Wessex on the main gate on the eastern side. Simply said, but deadly to actually put into action when the defenders were the Danish Great Army.

It was still early enough for dew to soak my boots as we marched on the walls. There was a smell of burning hanging over the city and the air was loud with birdsong, but soon the warning growl of the enemy's war horns began to echo over the land as we were spotted by Danish lookouts. I could clearly see that the breaches in the city's defences were blocked with stone-filled barrels and thorn brush and behind those was a wall of shields bristling with spears. This wasn't going to be easy.

My heart was racing as we walked forward, our own shields locked, while others formed a protecting roof against a hail of throwing axes and arrows. As usual the Danes were singing, their voices rolling around the sky fierce and heavy with the threat of their power.

Ethelred looked at me and grinned. I smiled back knowing such things are lucky before a battle. Somewhere high in the sky I could hear a lark's song, piercing through the deep voices of the Danes in a tumbling, trilling thrill of joy. I shouted aloud for the ferocious elation of battle that then suddenly rose up through me, and as Ethelred raised his sword we all leapt forward in a charge.

The steep embankment of the defences seemed to fall away as we ran, the Yellow Wyvern banner of Mercia snapping and rattling in the wind of our speed. We were heading for the widest breach in the palisade that topped the embankment. Here there was a dense row of stone-filled barrels and behind them stood the enemy, their shields tightly overlapping and deadly with spears and axes.

There was no time to think and we hit them with a roar. Ethelred leapt up on to the barricade of barrels and I immediately followed, my sword flashing and flickering as I killed again and again. Mouse leapt forward and over the line of shields, bringing down the Viking warriors and causing panic and alarm. Behind us the Mercians pressed forward bearing us up and over the barricade. We were in! We were in the city already!

The Great Army fell back in disciplined ranks, fighting a strong withdrawal as they backed down the steep embankment into the city proper. But now we had the advantage of high ground and we beat on their shields with everything we had. I called Mouse back and he took up his position protecting my left side.

Then even over the huge crescendo of our fighting we heard a great roar rise up into the air and we knew that the army of Wessex was attacking the main gates. We answered the sound with a powerful pulsing beat of our war chant:

"*OUT!* Out! Out!

"*OUT!* Out! Out!

"*OUT!* Out! Out!"

The simple syllable spat with fury and venom made the enemy give back one slow step at a time, though their discipline still held and they fought stubbornly making us pay for every step they gave us.

We were now in the streets of the city and suddenly the Danes melted away, falling back at speed before reforming their shield wall across the roadway that opened before us. Their line was anchored by the houses that stood on either side of the road, and I knew they'd be as stubborn to move as a limpet on a rock.

We hit them with a storm of swords, axes and spears but here they held their position and refused to give ground. Their voices rang out in a fierce battle-song once more and they pushed back against us. Their strength held us at bay and though we rallied and charged again and again, still they stood, defiant and mighty. But then I was suddenly aware of a black fury standing beside me and from it came the angry cawing of ravens. It was Ara, of course.

Her long skinny arms were raised above her head and her hands and fingers curled like claws as she spat words at the Danes. Her eyes were rolled back in her head so only the whites showed and saliva ran down her chin in a constant stream.

The enemy's singing stopped and they began to waver, but then a huge man leapt forward, a massive war hammer in his hand and a symbol of the thunder hammer around his neck. Here was a fighting priest of Thor and he smashed at our line with a massive fury and power, felling our soldiers like young saplings before the axe.

Now he stood before Ara herself and raising his hammer he ran forward, but the wise woman turned the whites of her eyes upon him, pointed a clawed finger and spat a word that exploded from her mouth in a shower of spit and blood. Immediately the man stopped and doubled up as though a blade had been driven into his guts. With a roar of defiance he straightened and raised his hammer again and this time Ara raised her hands and then suddenly snapped them down into a doubled fist. The man fell to his knees and the ravens flew in and drove their massive beaks into his eyes before rising up on a black flame of beating wings over the line of the Danes. The man fell forward on to his face and didn't move again.

Now the enemy began to give back, though still they maintained their wall and fought for every piece of ground. Ara marched with us, Ranhald and Raarken flying above her and her face contorted into a mask of fury and dark power.

In desperation the Danes began to throw flaming torches on to the roofs of the houses they passed so that soon the streets were filled with choking smoke and flying pieces of burning thatch.

We wrapped wet rags about our mouths and advanced, hacking down the enemy as we went. Ethelred still marched beside me, his face black with smoke and his teeth white and gleaming. I realised I must have looked as ludicrous and found myself laughing aloud in the midst of mayhem. Mouse was as smoke black as a 'shuck', the devil dog of legend, and as he ran in to attack, the line of the enemy's shields buckled as they fell back before his snarling threat.

At one point some of the Danes tried to outflank us by slipping through the side streets and suddenly appearing behind us, but raising my sword I took Mouse and led a charge against them, while the main body of our fighters continued to advance. We smashed through their shield wall as cleanly as a sharpened blade and cut them down in a brief blazing fury of fighting before joining our comrades again.

But now we had reached a wide square that I think must have been the 'moot', the great meeting place of the city. And then on the far side I saw the White Dragon banner of Wessex. I shouted aloud for joy. Father had breached the gate and was now driving the enemy before him!

We pushed the Great Army back into the square where once again they proved the greatness of their name by refusing to surrender, forming a massive shield wall and singing out their defiance. We fought for the rest of the day until at last we breached their wall and they began to fall in their hundreds before our swords and spears. Father then called out for a truce and offered terms. But still they refused to surrender and fought on desperately, falling in huge numbers to lie in the lake of blood that was slowly seeping into the soil of the city.

Again Father called on them to lay down their arms and at last a silence fell and the warriors of both sides stepped apart. Now it was that I saw Guthrum in the flesh for the first time. He was a giant of a man with yellow hair and beard that were streaked with grey, but despite his size and power, when he stepped out of the Great Army's ranks and Father pointed at the ground before him, this king of the Norsemen knelt and offered up his sword hilt first in final surrender. Then the rest of the Great Army did the same, falling to their knees and dropping their shields and weapons to the ground. A great cheer rose up from us filling the air with our fierce joy. THE GREAT ARMY WAS HUMBLED, THE GREAT ARMY WAS DEFEATED!

I turned and hugged Ethelred who still stood beside me and grinning broadly he suddenly kissed me. For a moment I forgot even Guthrum's surrender as my senses swam. But I am a fighting shield maiden of the Cerdingas, not some swooning girl, and I turned back to watch the Danes' capitulation. Even so, I linked my arm through Ethelred's. Sometimes it is necessary to claim one's own.

The enemy was allowed to march out of London and cross over the borders into the lands they called Danelaw. Hostages were given to ensure the peace and the Great Army was also made to leave behind all their weaponry, helmets, shields and mail shirts. When we watched them walking away through the wide valley of the Thames, they looked like a huge gathering of peasant farmers in their shirtsleeves, perhaps on their way to gather in the harvest. But they had no scythes or sickles.

Ara disappeared after the battle had been won, but I had no doubt she'd be back when least expected. Our casualties were heavy, with many dead, but the victory had been decisive. We would have peace ... for a while at least.

Edward had been wounded fighting to break through the main gates of the city, and had a deep scar just beneath his left eye. But he didn't mind: it was an honourable wound and made him look like the warrior he was. He'd fought on throughout the battle, his face a fearsome mask of blood. When I told him he was one of the bravest fighters I knew, he grinned happily and thanked me.

After that he joined me and Ethelred and the rest of our army in wild celebrations that lasted throughout the night.

XIII

Peace is a strange thing. In times of war you're desperate for it and pray for it every day. But when we finally had it in the year of our Lord 886, I'm ashamed to say that I felt bored. I think most intelligent people would be shocked if they knew how I felt, but here and there amongst the housecarles and soldiers I saw others who obviously felt the same as me.

I missed the excitement of the fighting. I missed my comrades in the shield wall, I missed the sense of power the battlefield gave me, and I missed the way the fear just fell away as the *joy* of combat filled me to the brim! I know all of this makes me sound like some sort of warmongering madwoman. In fact it makes me sound as bad as the worst sort of land-grabbing, home-burning pirate. I'm sure Guthrum himself would say exactly the same as me. But I wonder if he also felt the horror of seeing towns and villages in flames, and I also wonder if he felt bitter grief when friends died of battle wounds. Perhaps if the towns and villages were those of his own people he would feel horror. And perhaps if his friends died in battle he'd weep as much as I did for Cerdic, Father's old commander and war leader who I'd known since I was a little girl and who was killed in the battle for London.

This is war: a curse for any land and people, a destroyer of lives and civilisations, a completely evil and destructive force. But it's also a place where warriors find fame, where the deepest friendships and bonds are forged and where the very *sense* of what a country and a people actually are is made. From this war with the Danish Great Army, my father had made an idea of a new land, a land not of many small kingdoms, but one country with a shared language and culture. It wasn't made yet, and though the process had begun it wouldn't be finished for many years. But when it was, I was determined that it would be a country where everyone within it shared the same idea no matter where they or their families had originally been born.

It may be that I will help to make this land ... maybe. But at the moment there's peace and I am just Aethelflaed Cerdinga once more. I may train in the shield wall with my father's housecarles, but there's no war to test me to the very limits of my strength and bravery. I may keep myself battle-ready and alert, but I have no close comrade with whom I can share the danger of war and the joy of victory. And this isn't only because the war has ended, for now, but also because Ethelred has returned to his land of Mercia and he seems to have taken half of who I am with him. And now I'm left here in Wessex to be a daughter of the king in a time of peace.

Books filled some of my time, as did training and Mouse, but it was a relief when one morning I was summoned to meet Father in one of the council chambers. I thought that perhaps I was going to be allowed to sit in on some meeting about the building of another defensive burgh somewhere, or perhaps about improvement to the fyrd's training. But when I arrived the place was completely empty apart from

Father who was sitting at a small table in the middle of the floor.

He looked up when I walked in, but then returned to the papers he was reading and waved to the chair that stood next to his. I sat in silence and waited. The room seemed larger somehow without the ealdormen and advisors sitting on the benches that lined the walls, and I spent some time quietly watching flies circle in the shafts of sunlight that spilled through the small windows and from the vents in the roof.

" ... don't you think, Aethelflaed?"

"What?" I said, taken by surprise. Father had obviously been talking for some time and equally obviously I hadn't been listening.

"I said that now we have a time of peace for a while we ought to decide what you're going to do with your life," he explained patiently.

"Oh ... yes ... I suppose so," I answered.

"Normally your mother would have had this discussion with you, but unfortunately she's away in Mercia visiting relatives ... and also Ethelred."

The young ealdorman's name sharpened my senses and I concentrated more fully. "I suppose she'll be staying with him in the Mercian palace in Tamworth."

"Yes," Father agreed. "In fact, she's gone to lay a proposition before him, one that I know he'll accept and be pleased with."

A dog barked down in the courtyard below and I automatically looked towards the window and laid my hand on Mouse's collar as he got ready to reply.

"Aethelflaed, are you listening to me?"

I turned to face him squarely. "Yes, Father, please carry on."

"Good, because it's been decided that you should marry Ethelred and seal the alliance between Mercia and Wessex."

"Yes, Father, I know."

"You know?"

"Yes. It's the obvious thing to do and I'm the obvious choice to do it with. Handing London over to Mercian control after we'd liberated it from the Danes was a master stroke of diplomacy on your part and I'm the cream that makes the apple pie complete, if I may say so."

Father's eyes were as round as the new coins showing him in battledress that he'd recently had minted. But then he threw back his head and laughed until his voice echoed throughout the chamber.

"And how do you feel about this, my young mistress of diplomacy?" he eventually asked.

I thought for a while, then said, "Satisfied and contented. Ethelred's a good man, an equally good ruler and a great soldier. It also helps that he's young and easy on the eye. Once the alliance is cemented, the borders will be safe for generations to come ... at least *ours* will be. I'm saying nothing about those of so-called Danelaw. Besides, I've decided I love Ethelred, and I think he loves me. But if he doesn't, then I've also decided that he soon will. So what else can come of this marriage but good things for the people of Wessex and Mercia and for Aethelflaed and Ethelred?"

Father looked ready to laugh again, but he controlled himself and merely smiled. "Good. Then we can look forward to a wedding as soon as may be."

"We can," I agreed.

After I left the chamber I went to the stables and had my horse saddled, then I rode out into the countryside that surrounds Winchester, the capital of Wessex. When I was clear of the usual carts, wagons and other traffic that flowed to and from the city, I kicked the horse to a gallop and thundered along the road singing for joy and laughing aloud while Mouse added his huge barks to the noise and weaved from side to side across the road ahead of me.

But then I spied a dark figure standing in the exact centre of the route and I slowed to a trot. When I was near enough Ara stepped forward and looked into my face.

"You're pleased with your fate then, Aethelflaed Cerdinga?"

"Yes," I answered simply.

The wise woman nodded. "Your life will be one of fighting and fame. Are you ready for it?"

"Yes," I said again and suddenly the sky was filled with the calling voices of ravens and the black fire of their wings as Ranhald and Raarken leapt into flight.

Historical Note

The precise dating of Anglo-Saxon history is fraught with difficulty. Often the original sources don't bother with exact dates at all or, if they do, they may contradict those given by other supposedly authoritative texts.

The date for the Danish attack on Chippenham that drove King Alfred and his family into exile, for example, varies between AD 876 and AD 878. The same can be said for the birth date of the principal character of our tale: Aethelflaed, the daughter of the king. This meanders between AD 868 and AD 872. In fact, I found one reference to her being born in AD 864 – which was actually before her parents were married. This would have been a very unlikely happening at the time!

However, we can be confident in the facts of Aethelflaed's later life. She married Ethelred of Mercia and, after her father died, she campaigned against the Danes, along with Edward her brother – who became King of Wessex after Alfred the Great's death – and Ethelred. Together they re-conquered the Viking lands known as Danelaw. Then, when Ethelred was no longer able to rule Mercia (either because of illness or because of injuries sustained in battle; again, the sources are unclear), she ruled in his stead as 'The Lady of the Mercians', becoming Queen in all but name.

In AD 918, the powerful Danish rulers of Jorvik (now known as York) sent peace envoys to her, acknowledging her as their overlord. Before they arrived, though, she died – some say of wounds received in battle just days before.

Bonus Bits!

Who's who?

Can you match the name of each character with their role? (The answers are at the end of this section – no peeking, though!)

1. Aethelflaed
2. Edward
3. Ara
4. Alfred
5. Aethelfryth
6. Cerdic Guthweinson

a. King of Wessex
b. Commander of guards
c. King's eldest daughter
d. King's only son
e. King's youngest daughter
f. Royal nursemaid

Who was King Alfred the Great?

Alfred the Great was an Anglo-Saxon king between AD 871 and AD 899. He defended England against a Danish invasion and founded the first ever English navy.

He was also responsible for the creation of The Anglo-Saxon Chronicle, a collection of historical records written in Old English. This helped to revive learning and encouraged the use of the English language at a time when most records were written in Latin or ancient Greek. The book also ensured that Alfred's achievements were recorded, so we know more about him than about any other Anglo-Saxon king.

Who were the Anglo-Saxons?

The Anglo-Saxons were warriors who were also farmers. They came from north-west Europe and first began to invade Britain when the Romans were in control.

They were great fighters and were very fierce if you were unlucky enough to be up against them. They were also very good at hunting, farming, making cloth and working with leather.

And who were the Danes – or the 'Vikings'?

The name 'Viking' means 'pirate raid'. The Vikings were often Danes: many came from Denmark, while others were from Norway and Sweden. The Vikings invaded Britain and Ireland and tried to take Anglo-Saxon land and treasures.

Understanding the historical jargon!

There are lots of words in this book that are specific to Anglo-Saxon times (which is hardly surprising, as the story is set in those times!). This list might help you if you get stuck.

brazier – simple cooking device, a bit like a barbeque, with coals in the bottom and a grill on which food (usually meat) would be cooked

burgh – town

byrnie – piece of armour that covered the neck and shoulders of a soldier

chamberlain – person who looked after the household of a king or nobleman

ealdorman – high-ranking royal official of an Anglo-Saxon region

fyrd – part-time soldiers who also had non-military jobs

garrison – group of soldiers stationed in a fortress or town for defence

housecarle – bodyguard of a king or nobleman

insignia – badge or emblem

metropolis – capital or main city of a country or a region

Norseman – someone who spoke what is now known as Old Norse between the 8th and 11th centuries AD

overlord – land-owning lord who allowed others to live on his land in return for their work

pagan – person who believes in lots of different gods

palisade – a fence of wooden stakes or iron railings

scullion – servant who did the worst kitchen jobs

thegn – noble or military courtier of a king or nobleman, below an ealdorman in rank

What does that mean?

There are some other uncommon words in this book, too. This list might help you if you get stuck.

cavernous – like a cavern or cave in size and shape

etiquette – rules for polite behavior

incantations – words intended as magic spells or charms

invincible – unbeatable

maiming – wounding someone in a way that means their body is permanently damaged

parried – evaded attack using a weapon as a countermove

treacherous – guilty of betrayal

What next?

This story is written from the viewpoint of an Anglo-Saxon king's daughter. How does she make us view the Danes? How would this be different if the story were written from the viewpoint of a Danish king's daughter? Why not do some research and choose part of the story to write from the viewpoint of the Danes?

Answers to 'Who's Who?'

1c   2d   3f   4a   5e   6b

Look out for
these other
exciting stories
from history!

ISBN: 9781472918093

When the young Celt Lucan sees a legion
of Roman soldiers near his village it definitely
makes sense to hide. But hiding in a wagon
could prove to be a dangerous mistake . . .

Follow Lucan's hilarious adventures as he
tries to escape the dreaded Romans.

ISBN: 9781472925893   ISBN: 9781472925923

Join brothers Arthur and Finn as they travel back
to ancient Egypt, where they try to prevent a
kidnapping and stop a war; and to ancient Greece,
to try and impress the Spartan king and avoid
the wrath of the Persian Army.